C000121429

Full
Fathom
Five

Mike Wilson

Biscuit Publishing

For Alan
Best Wishes
M Wilson

Published by Biscuit Publishing Ltd., 2005

Copyright © Mike Wilson 2005

ISBN 1-903914-19-1

A catalogue for this book is
available from the British Library

First published in Great Britain by
Biscuit Publishing Ltd., 2005
PO Box 123, Washington,
Newcastle upon Tyne
NE37 2YW

Second impression March 2005

Front cover from a painting by Barry Reigate ©

Printed and bound in Great Britain by
Jasprint Ltd., Tyne & Wear

Mike Wilson is Bridlington born and bred. Apart from 15 years in Maidenhead and Aylesbury, Mike has lived and worked in Driffield and Bridlington, in the East Riding of Yorkshire.

 He was inspired to write by his experiences in the Bridlington Town Play, *Come Hell or High Water*, in 1995, in which he was privileged to take the role of Kit Brown.

Since then Mike has portrayed Kit Brown on many occasions, particularly in Bridlington's Harbour Heritage Museum. He has written articles about his life, and this work of "faction" hopefully brings Kit's story to a wider audience.

Now retired from a working life as a typesetter on newspapers and magazines, Mike is currently the Chairman of the National Association of Writers' Groups, for whom he edits and typesets their magazine *Link*. He has had successes in writing competitions, for short stories, poetry and one-act plays. His local history articles have been published in local, regional and national magazines.

Mike lives with his wife Diane, still in Bridlington.

4

This book is dedicated to the memory of Bridlington lifeboatmen of the past and to those who continue to serve on the town's lifeboats.

I also dedicate this book to Remould Theatre, writers, backstage staff and players of *Come Hell or High Water*, for providing such a liberating experience.

And, of course, the book is dedicated to my wife Diane. It is doubtful that I would have ever soared to these dizzying heights of achievement, without her unfailing support and love.

The telling of this story owes a great debt to the work of Rupert Creed and Richard Hayhow, the creators of *Come Hell or High Water*. The author acknowledges that any similarity between this work and the Bridlington Town Play is due entirely to his admiration of their contribution to the history of Bridlington and its fishing and lifeboat communities.

I would like to thank all those who have encouraged me to write, even those who said I'd never be a writer, but especially members of Bridlington Writers' Group who supported me in many ways as I wrote this story.

Thanks are also due to staff at Bridlington Library for access to the Bridlington Room and all those who have made even the slightest contribution to the production of this book.

I'd like to thank Robert Edrick, whose one-day workshop fired the spark to ignite this conflagration.

To Brian Lister of Biscuit Publishing, my thanks for having faith in me and this story.

Full Fathom Five Thy Father Lies

Full fathom five thy father lies,
　Of his bones are coral made,
Those are pearls that were his eyes:
　Nothing of him that doth fade,
But doth suffer a sea-change
Into something rich and strange.
Sea-nymphs hourly ring his knell:
Hark! Now I hear them, ding-dong, bell.

The Tempest, William Shakespeare

Full
Fathom
Five

Mike Wilson

Chapter 1

28 March 1898

"Is Dad coming home *tonight*, Mam?"

Mary Brown pulled her scarf round her neck then blew into her gloves as she shivered in the bitter north-easterly that swept Bridlington Bay. She drew her daughter Kitty closer. "Whisht, bairn."

Through flakes of snow they peered into the gloom, hoping to catch a glimpse of Kit.

"But is it tonight, Mam? *Tonight*?"

Mary's older children knew they had lost him, but she had returned again to wait at the end of the pier. "Just in case," she told them. But her heart sank as with her mind's eye she saw Kit – Christopher, her husband – fighting the sea on that wild freezing night three days earlier when the lifeboats had been launched in a terrible gale. Mary was still certain he would come home.

As dusk became night, Mary hummed the tune of *Eternal Father*, then started to sing, "O hear me when I cry to Thee, my man's in peril on the sea." Her voice became louder as she sang out the words. Louder, then louder until they became a howl of despair.

Kitty sobbed and clung to her mother.

Mary's scream dropped to a sigh, then to silence. She looked towards the chalk of Flamborough Head seven miles to the north-east where the lighthouse flashed its warnings. She then turned to gaze all the way south to where the dunes edged the sea. There was nothing to be seen but black sea and darkness. The only sound was the crashing of waves against the pierhead, accented by squawking herring gulls. In her nostrils were scents of the harbour: fish, wet rope, seaweed and the rawness of the sea. And, on her lips, the taste of salt: the wind-swept spray – and tears.

Hardly visible from the *Coble & Anchor* inn on the harbour top, Mary's dark shape trudged slowly up the pier. Half-way along, she stopped, turned to the sea and shouted "Christopher!" The last syllable became a sob.

Two men walked down the pier towards her. Her son Frank took her arm and escorted her towards the road, while Fred, her elder son, watched his mother's face as he walked beside them. Kitty reached to hold Fred's hand.

At the foot of the steps which led to the road, Mary and her sons were joined by two smaller figures which emerged from a doorway among the fishermen's huts on the pier. Mary's older daughters, Eliza and Maud, had cried as many tears as their mother at Kit's loss, but neither felt able to walk with their mother to the pierhead. Mary had not insisted. She respected her daughters' wishes, despite her loneliness.

"Come on, Mam," said Eliza, reaching for Mary's fingers. "Here, Kitty," she added, and offered her hand to the five-year-old.

"Let's go home," said Maud, putting her arm around her mother's waist.

"Aye," said Mary, "Your dad will be wanting his supper when he comes in. It'll be high water soon and he always comes back on the tide."

The young women exchanged glances with their brothers but said nothing and nestled closer to Mary as they walked slowly up the steps. Huddling below the street were the harbourmaster's office, the chandlery, the workshops where Harry sewed his sails and Silas the boatbuilder constructed cobles with the finest timber from Boynton Woods. At the top of the steps they turned to walk towards the cottages at the foot of Spring Pump Slipway.

In the *Coble & Anchor*, Jess Brown was making himself heard about the incident which had robbed him of a brother.

"They should never have launched. Tide were all

wrong. What with the seas smashing against the wall and that gale pushing t'waves towards t'Cut, the boat was in danger all along. Kit tried telling them, but, nay, they wouldn't have it." He brandished his beer mug like a weapon at the other fishermen in the bar. "It were a waste of a good man," he continued. "There'll never be another 'un like our Kit."

"Aye, thoo may be right. He didn't have to die. Yon boat weren't in real danger. I heard it were only showing flag for a pilot." A stocky man with a heavily bearded face made its way to the front of the group. "It's a pity them men didn't listen to Kit."

"And now there's our Mary robbed of a husband. God knows what'll happen to her and the bairn now those lasses of hers are wed." Jess once again used his glass to emphasise his feelings.

"I saw her going to the pierhead. She's still waiting for him." Benjamin Pockley, a younger man, spoke in a quieter voice.

"Fair turns me over when I hear her shouting for Kit," Jess said, a slight shudder rumbling over his shoulders. "The sea got him, but she won't accept it. Even my Maggie can't get it through to her. She won't talk about a funeral till he's found, but the vicar up at t'Priory says he'll do the best for him when he comes home."

"Our lass has tried to help her face it, but nowt she says does any good." Benjamin Pockley came to the front to address the men. "I don't think Mary realises that Kit's our hero as well as hers. She wants him for herself. It's not the way we do it in Bridlington."

There was a general murmuring of agreement, and glasses were raised to swallow another mouthful of beer.

"But we know how it happened, don't we? Those reckless youngsters. Wouldn't listen." Charlie Simpson's normally pale face was suffused with anger. He swallowed the rest of his pint, turned to the bar, and shouted: "I'll have another o' them, Clem," and threw some copper onto the counter.

"No, it weren't just that. Tide were too high and Kit were right. I heard him telling them not to launch. Him and Dick Purvis are no fools. They knew it were too dangerous. They should have waited an hour. Tide would have been off the wall." Jess Brown commanded his audience with his authority, and heads nodded.

"It's all right you talking about waiting." Faces turned to the corner of the bar, where Robert Hopper sat, his heavily bandaged leg stretched out on a stool. "But you weren't called a coward after the *Bordeaux* sank. That hurt that did. And Captain Atkin didn't help either. Look, we wanted to go as soon as we realised there was a boat in danger, but no, there was dithering and indecision again. No wonder some folk think Brid's a laughing stock, and that we don't have a real lifeboat service at all."

Robert took another gulp of his ale, and continued: "I were lucky. Jack Creaser dragged me out of the sea and up them steps. You all know that. But we launched the boats because we had to prove we weren't cowards. It were no good coxswain and the Captain telling us to be calm and wait. We wanted to go. We had to go."

"I heard the lifeboats hadn't even been officially called out." Everyone turned towards another corner and saw Dick Purvis drinking his pint. "Some hothead youths fired by rum said they wanted to be heroes – like their dads."

"But," shouted a different voice, "we can't do anything about the past. And we can't do anything about Kit till his body turns up. And you know this bay. It could be months."

"I reckon it'll never turn up. It'll be out on Smithwick Sands and it'll stay there for ever," called another man.

The *Coble & Anchor* was small, at the end of a terrace. Its street door came directly onto Queens Square where it overlooked the harbour waters. A board on the wall declared that the inn had once been part of a building in which Queen Henrietta Maria of England had hidden for nine days. The room in which the men had assembled to discuss the incident yet again was packed. The hubbub increased as the men put forward their theories. Occasionally a voice became distinct for a few seconds. On three of the walls, gas burners flared, hissing and spluttering, moving shadows round the room in fits and starts.

The street door burst open, banging against the wall, and a youth appeared, puffing and panting with exertion. "They've found him, they've found him," he shouted, gesticulating towards the sea. "Kit Brown's been found."

The room became a maelstrom of bodies, as fishermen swallowed their drinks, grabbed at coats and mufflers, and squeezed out of the door onto the street.

"Where, lad? Where?" Ben Pockley asked.

"Down at Hornsea," the youth replied, pointing south.

Once outside the men charged down the street to the harbour steps. A ragged file of dark-coated men swept to the door of the harbourmaster's office, the fastest having the right to bang on the door.

"Open up Alf. Open up!" Charlie Simpson hammered on the door with a tight fist. He banged again and the door opened.

A man with a pale face glared at Charlie, and said: "What's the hell's up?"

"What have you heard? About Kit? Have you found him?" Shouts could be heard in different voices as the men wanted answers.

"I know what you know," replied Alf. "Someone's sent word from Hornsea to say he's been found, and that's it."

"Come on, you're the harbourmaster, you must know more." Benjamin Pockley took a step nearer Alf. "Who found him?"

Alfred Stephenson held his hands apart as though in defence. "I heard that some young lad found a body in the water at Hornsea and it's presumed it's Kit. But we don't know for sure. I'm waiting for the Captain then we're off to see if it's him."

"I'll come too," said Benjamin.

"Aye, me too."

"But we can't all go. We'll send a message back when we have news."

The crowd quietened and faces turned as the men parted to allow a squat man with a walking stick to approach the door. Captain Thomas Atkin, the lifeboat secretary at Bridlington, limped to the front of the crowd.

"Ey up, Alf. Are you ready? We've twelve miles to go, you know." He totally ignored the agitated men.

"Yes, Captain, that I am," replied Alf, who closed his door and locked it.

The two men walked through the group of fishermen towards a horse and trap a few yards away.

"So they've found Kit. At last," Benjamin Pockley said, more to himself than to the others.

"Now we can have a funeral and perhaps our Mary will find some peace," Jess Brown replied.

A handful of men on the beach at Hornsea clustered in the light of a guttering oil lamp round the body of a man wearing a dark blue knitted guernsey and black trousers. One foot was bare, the other still wearing its hob-nailed boot and black sock. The body had been dragged from the waves and had left a trail on the sand.

Captain Atkin and Alf Stephenson strode along the sands towards the group, which stood aside from the corpse as they approached.

Alf and the Captain peered into the expressionless face of the body.

"It's Kit," said Alf, gulping back the taste of bile, as the light from his lamp played harsh shadows over the face of the corpse.

"Aye," agreed the Captain. He looked up at the men: "We'll take him now. Thank you all for looking after him. Help us get him into the trap."

Alf turned to the group and asked: "Who found him?"

"Young Johnny Slater, sir. A fisherman's lad digging

for bait early on," a man in the crowd volunteered. "He's about here somewhere."

A boy of about eleven ran up to the group and shouted: "I found him, sir. I found him. He was waving to me from the waves so I waded out to help him."

Alf Stephenson and Captain Atkin turned to each other: "Waving?"

"Aye, sir, waving. Like this." The boy flung an arm from one side of his body to the other.

"Sorry, lad, but that was the sea. He were past waving." Alf put his hand on the boy's shoulder to comfort him.

"Oh," said the boy, lowering his head as sorrow filled his eyes.

"But, young man, there is a reward for the discovery of this body. Did you know? Ten guineas has been offered by the folk at Bridlington for the recovery of Kit Brown. If you found him I reckon you should get the reward. What do you think, Captain?"

"Agreed," and the Captain gave a slight nod.

"So, lad, ten guineas. What do you think of that?" Alf smiled and the boy's face beamed.

"Well, sir, I'll be rich, won't I? Ten guineas!"

"Aye, that's a grand start for a young lad like you. And what do you want to be when you're grown up?"

The lad thrust out his chest and his spindly frame reached its full four feet three inches. Pride shone in his eyes as he gazed up at the Captain. "A lifeboatman, sir. A lifeboatman."

Chapter 2

23 December 1893

"A lifeboatman? You? A lifeboatman? You're far too impulsive." Kit Brown turned away from his son and continued filling two barrels with water in a corner of his warehouse near the cottage on Spring Pump Slipway.

The previous evening, Kit Brown had visited the butcher at the Quay. "Now then, Mr Jenkins. You'll not have any beef left?" Kit posed the question as though he expected a negative answer. When Mr Jenkins said he still had some meat to sell, Kit said: "That'll be no good come Monday. I'll take what you have. How much are you going to charge me for that?"

The butcher and Kit haggled a price and Kit agreed to let him have fish to that value. Using a small handcart he took the meat back to his warehouse. He had previously half filled two barrels with water. He put a potato in each barrel and then poured in salt until the potatoes came to the top and floated. Kit then added the beef until the barrels were packed. He was able to keep as much as a hundredweight in each. Kit exchanged fish for meat as a way of improving the family diet.

Kit had two barrels containing beef and one with pork, several others stuffed with herring, and one or two, unmarked, set to one side. No-one in the family mentioned those.

"Impulsive? What do yer mean, too impulsive!" Fred Brown spluttered.

"What I said. Too impulsive! You'll never get anything right behaving like that. Pass some more beef," Kit continued working, wrists plunged into the barrel.

"But I got a medal same as you." Fred's anger spilled over and he thumped the meat onto a bench which ran along one wall of the warehouse.

Kit stood erect. "Aye, lad, that you did. But them as gave you it never heard the full story, did they? No-one told them that you clambered on board the *Victoria* without a rope holding the boats. You could have fallen and been crushed to death. Either that or drowned."

"But I wasn't, Dad, that's the point," Fred said in an effort to lessen the conflict. He picked up another roll of beef from the handcart.

"But it is the point, Fred. You can't go charging about if you intend doing any good. You have to think. Just a moment's thought would have told you to make sure the boats were tied before you went up and over. Another minute wouldn't have made happorth of difference." Kit added another joint to the barrel.

"But it might, Dad. *Victoria* sank just as the last man came aboard the *Swiftsure*, didn't she? We only just made it." He slowed his voice down and stood up straight to accentuate his words. "I reckon getting on board quick was what saved them men."

"You went on board on your own. Tom and Jack went after the boats had been tied. If you'd waited a minute, three could have gone searching together. But because we were still struggling with the boats, it took us twice as long." Kit paused. "There's a right way and a wrong way, Fred, and being impulsive is the wrong way. One day you'll learn that. *And* remember I told you." Kit pushed the last of the meat into the salted water and fitted a lid.

"But you're always telling me what to do. I want to do things my way, I know what I'm doing. And I say I'm old enough for the lifeboat crew."

"Look lad," Kit Brown put a hand on his son's shoulders. Fred stood an inch taller than his father. "You haven't the experience yet. Get a couple more years on you, and we'll see."

Fred's shoulders slumped.

"But I'll tell you what. I'll tell Atkin to put your name down so you can start next year."

Fred turned away. He muttered: "But he's as old as you are, and won't understand."

As Fred left the warehouse, Kit's thoughts went back to that fearful night weeks earlier on board the *Swiftsure*.

On board the *Swiftsure*, five pairs of eyes peered into the night to recapture the flare of the stricken boat. The men knew she was there but for now the clouds had hidden her from view. Snow flurries burst over the *Swiftsure* in pockets of freezing gusts.

"Don't you think it's a bit over bad for a coble, Kit?" Jack Usher shouted, as another wave spilt into the boat.

"We can always turn back if it gets too bad. We've come this far. Might as well carry on," Kit gripped the tiller and kept his eye on the sails of the *Swiftsure*.

"She's there, Dad!" Fred Brown pointed ahead a few points to port, and the spluttering lamp of the stricken boat could be seen through the clouds.

"Aye, lad! I've got her!" Kit leaned on the tiller and the coble thrashed through the oncoming rollers.

As the coble drew closer to the briganteen, the men could see her painted name at the stern: *Victoria*. Despite the surging of the waves between the vessels, Kit brought *Swiftsure* within a foot of the wallowing ship.

While Kit clung to the tiller, the three older men held ropes ready to throw over to the *Victoria*. They shouted "Ahoy, there!" but there was no response. The coble slid along the briganteen from stern to prow but no-one could be seen.

Fred Brown, bursting with excitement, clambered on the planks at the side of the coble, and waited until the briganteen swung towards him after the next wave. As the space between the boats lessened, he leapt upwards to grab the gunwales of the larger boat. With a shout, he swung himself over and turned to look down into the coble at his father.

"Come on, come on!" And then he was gone. The men in the coble tied their ropes, securing the two boats. Tom

18

Clark and Jack Usher clambered over the gunwales of the *Victoria* and disappeared from Kit's view.

The door of the galley of the *Victoria* burst open to his thump and Fred Brown saw the cook lying exhausted on a pile of rope. The man's eyes peered about him as he heard the footsteps. Fred Brown reached down and dragged him to his feet. "Come on, sailor. I'll soon have you safe." He grabbed the man and slung him over his shoulder. Weaving up the steps and onto the deck of the pitching *Victoria*, Fred clung to the rails as he made his way back towards the *Swiftsure*. He looked down into the coble and shouted: "Here's a passenger for you, Dad!" Kit Brown and Dick Purvis grabbed the rescued man's legs and lowered him into the coble.

The two men looked up towards Fred but saw only his back as he disappeared again.

Fred found Jack and Tom in the wheelhouse, hoisting two more sailors to their shoulders.

"Fred, get the captain. He's still in there!" Jack shouted.

"OK," Fred replied as he dashed across the deck. In the wheelhouse, the captain was clinging to the wheel. Fred couldn't see how he was still standing, but then saw the rope around his waist. He slashed through the rope with his knife, and the captain dropped into Fred's arms. Fred looked into the glazed eyes of the man and said: "It's all right, Captain. You're safe now."

Fred hoisted the man onto his shoulder and made his way to the deck and then to the gunwales. He shouted: "That's them all!" and hands reached for the captain to lower him gently into the bottom of the coble.

Fred jumped from the larger boat and clapped both Jack and Tom on their shoulders, shouting: "Well done, well done!"

"OK, lads, let's go!" Kit shouted. As soon as the men were secured aboard the coble, the restraining ropes were unfastened, Kit pushed the tiller to starboard and the boats separated.

As the rescuers turned to look back at the *Victoria*, a wave smashed into her, and, with a groan of shattered timbers, she turned over and sank.

The five fishermen looked at each other, then at the men they had rescued. "Let's get home," Kit said. The faces of the rescued men showed their astonishment at being grabbed from the prospect of a watery grave.

The storm was still at its height and the waves, cheated from their prey, battered the coble as it sped towards harbour. Spray crashed into the bottom of the boat, where the rescued men spluttered and moaned. With Kit at the the tiller and the four other men ready for whatever the sea threw at them, the coble neared the harbour entrance.

At the Canch, a sandbank across the entrance to the harbour, the waves were breaking in a maelstrom. Waves bounced back from the harbour walls, creating huge pillars of water across the harbour mouth. Using all his skill, Kit steered the boat through the agitated surf until the coble was in safe waters.

The five men looked at each other. "Bloody hell, Dick lad, that were risky," Jack Usher said, starting to lower the mainsail as the coble ran up to the landing stage steps. Tom Clark and Dick Purvis manhandled the rudder aboard, tied the boat up and watched as the rescued men climbed out onto solid ground.

"Aye, it was that. I've never seen the sea like that before. I'm glad Kit was with us." Dick Purvis shook hands with the captain of the *Victoria*, and said: "Glad we were there to help."

The captain replied: "You saved our lives. What else can we say?"

The rescued men were helped up the steps to the harbour top.

"What now, Kit?" asked Dick Purvis.

"Let's get them to John Grantham's. He'll find a bed for them. They need a hot meal. Then we'll get off home." Kit put his arm across the shoulder of the *Victoria*'s captain and led him up the street from the harbour.

At the *Waterloo Café*, Kit banged on the door. "Open up, John. We've customers for you!"

Within two minutes a window on the first floor opened, and a head appeared, shouting: "What's going on? Who is it?"

"It's Kit Brown, John. We've some sailors needing a meal and a bed. Open up!"

The upstairs window closed and then the street door opened. John Grantham looked at the bedraggled men in front of him, opened the door wider and beckoned them in.

"Right, John," said Kit. "A hot meal and a bed for them. Shipwrecked Sailors will pay. I'll see to it in the morning. I'm to my bed."

The rescued men followed John Grantham into the warmth of the café, while Kit turned to his crewmates and said: "Right, lads. A good job there, I reckon. Let's away home."

"Aye. Goodnight Kit." John Grantham closed the door.

Dick Purvis, Tom Clark and Jack Usher accompanied Kit and Fred to the top of the slope to the Brown's cottage on Spring Pump Slipway, where the group parted.

As Kit walked alongside his son down the cobbled road, he felt a hand on his shoulder.

"Wow, Dad! That was amazing! To be in a rescue like that, well, I wonder if I'll ever do anything like that again!"

"Don't say that, lad! You want to pray to God you never have to!"

Chapter 3

10 February 1871

"They're launching the *Harbinger*!" Kit Brown ran into his harbourside cottage, shouting.

Mary's hands flew to her mouth in shock. "Don't go, Kit!" she said, rushing towards him.

"Look, lass," Kit said, holding her at arm's length and looking straight into her eyes. "I must."

"But Kit, you've done your bit for the lifeboat. Let someone else do it."

"I have to go. There's ships in danger. And the storm's getting worse. Things must be bad if they're taking the fishermen's boat." Kit started to drag on his seaboots.

"You're exhausted. You were out all day yesterday."

"I've had a night's rest."

"Oh, Kit, if you go, I'll be worrying my guts out for you."

"I know that, lass. And my being sorry doesn't help. But it's expected. I know it always seems to be me. But you know I'm expected to turn up. I'm part of the lifeboat crew."

"There's always enough crew for the *Harbinger*, Kit. You know that. It's never *not* gone out. And there's the National boat, too."

"Look, Mary, our boat is the one the town cares for." He wrapped his neckerchief round his throat then put on his serge jacket. "You know how many locals will be out there to help us. They're shouting for men now. Listen."

And, carried on the gale, came a shout from outside: "We need more men!"

"I can hear them, Kit, and I'm telling you again. I don't want you to go."

The shout outside was repeated: "We need more men!"

"Pass us that oilskin, lass. I'm off."

"Get your own damned oilskin." Mary stamped her foot and walked to the other side of the table.

"You watch your language, Mary Brown."

"I'll not help you to go again."

"Pass that oilskin, Mary!"

"I'm sick of it, Kit." She stamped again. "That damned boat always comes first. For once put your family before that thing. Them kids upstairs daren't speak when the weather's bad. They dread it. They think one day you'll not come back. And a dead father's no good to them."

"I've always come back, lass. Always will."

"So you say, but that storm out there's the worst we've ever seen. You've not had enough rest. You know how bad it can be in the Bay. If you go out now you could get yourself drowned."

"I know how to look after myself. The damned sea hasn't got me yet." Kit's anger grew at Mary's delay.

"But Kit, the first time would be your last. For God's sake, man, think of others for a change."

"Think of others!" Kit shouted. "How dare you! I *am* thinking of others when I'm out in that boat. That's the only reason I go 'cos my mind's on others. Those poor sailors freezing cold and drowning. That's why I go out. Why else do you think I do it? There's precious little brass in it for t'bairns. Every time I get hold of those oars my guts turn to lead. A great roaring pounds my brain and it's not just the crash of the waves. You don't think I'm being heroic out there, do you?" Kit smashed his fist on the table, making the crockery jangle. "My God, woman, you must be crazy if you think that. There's sweat flooding down my back with fear, sweat streaming into my eyes, and with that and spray and snow I can hardly see a damned thing, my back's blazing, I'm frozen wet through and you've seen the blisters on my hands. So don't reckon on I do it 'cos I like it."

"Kit!" Mary backed away from Kit as he stormed across the floor, his voice raised.

"I've never telled thee all this before, 'cos I've not

23

wanted to scare thee. But you must know it's no fun out there. For any of us. But at least *Harbinger*'s a sound boat with fine men in the crew. I've someone to come home to, but them poor beggars out there – unless we get to them first, well, all they've got is a watery grave."

Mary reached behind her, then turned to Kit. Her voice was quiet: "Here's your oilskin, Kit. I'll pray for you."

Kit took the oilskin and pulled it over his shoulders: "Thanks, lass." He went to Mary and took her in his arms. "Give us a kiss and I'll go."

Chapter 4

10 February 1871

Kit Brown trembled with cold. Barely able to move or think, he felt himself being lifted out of the lifeboat. He realised he was on the frozen sands half a mile from Bridlington harbour. His hands leaked blood and his eyebrows and beard were caked with crystals of snow driven by gale-force south-east winds. His clothing was saturated with freezing sea water.

Mary Brown held out a blanket and he all but fell into its warmth. He felt her arms go round his body. "Thanks, Mary," he said, shuddering, teeth chattering.

"Oh Kit, are you all right?" she said, rubbing Kit's arms with her hands. "You're frozen. Come on, let's get you into warm clothes. There's some meat stew on the go at home." She helped Kit to stumble along the beach to the steps leading to the roadway above.

"No, lass. I ought to stay. There's other ships out there wanting help. I'm needed on *Harbinger*." Kit tried to move Mary's hands away, but she clung on.

"You've done enough. Someone else will have to go. You've done your bit. Come on." Mary continued to rub her hands up and down Kit's arms. Kit pulled the blanket tighter round his body and said: "I'm so cold, Mary."

The scene had been replayed several times that morning, as lifeboatmen were lifted from the *Harbinger*. She was a small wooden rowing lifeboat, with a crew of nine, eight men at the oars and another at the tiller.

The storm engulfing Bridlington Bay was the worst for many years. It sprang up overnight, the winds veering from north-west to south-east. At first the winds blew gently but they increased to gale force, and a sudden drop in temperature brought flurries of snow and sleet.

The Royal National Lifeboat Institute boat *Robert Whitworth* rescued many sailors before it was withdrawn from service. The crew found it too heavy and unwieldy in the conditions that morning. The *Harbinger*, a smaller lighter boat, made seven trips to save lives. She returned to the beach, her crew exhausted, battered by the winds and waves, blinded by the snow and sleet, frozen by the bitter cold, bleeding from hauling on reluctant oars.

Many of the crew were allowed to creep home for warmth and food. But now other men were needed to man the boat. And a cry was heard along the sands of Bridlington: "We need more men!"

Chapter 5

10 February 1871

"We need more men!" John Robinson, cox of the *Harbinger* lifeboat, shouted from the prow of the boat. The *Harbinger* had been pulled up the sands out of the reach of the sea as its exhausted crew was allowed to rest. The experienced men, who had been been out up to seven times, stumbled their way to their cottages for a rest, food and a change of clothes. Before the day was out, they would be back to fight those terrible waves.

Men in the crowd shuffled their feet in indecision. Their wives nudged them gently at first, then roughly, in an endeavour to persuade them to volunteer. But the stooped, shuddering men who had left the boat a few minutes earlier were hardly an inspiration.

Once more John Robinson hollered, "We need more men!"

He gazed into the crowd gathered on the safety of the beach and sought a familiar face. But there was none. "I need another crew! There's lives to be saved out there!"

The crowd in front of Robinson parted and two men strode towards him. A whisper in the crowd blossomed into a shout: "It's Purdon! David Purdon!"

David Purdon shouted up to Robinson: "I'll volunteer. And John Clappison will come with me."

John Robinson shook hands with Purdon as he clambered into the *Harbinger*. "Well, you'll know the boat as well as anybody, I suppose. Thanks."

David Purdon sat down in the boat he had built. Funded by a Hungarian count, the *Harbinger* was crewed by local fishermen. She was of a flatter build than the RNLI boat, and better for the coastal waters of Bridlington Bay. She was light and manoeuvrable and she handled the surf conditions well. The *Harbinger* was not just a lifeboat;

she was used as a harbour boat by the harbourmaster, and she assisted with pilot duties in the bay. She was maintained by the Sailors' and Workingmen's Club on Cliff Street, only a few yards from the cottage on Spring Pump Slipway where Kit Brown was thawing out in front of the fire.

David was joined by John Clappison, his assistant in the boatyard in North Street. Both men were experienced in boat-building, many of the cobles in the harbour having begun their days in the North Street yard.

"We need more men!" John Robinson's call rang out again. Within a few minutes, six more men had clambered aboard, taking their places at the oars.

"OK, let's go!" John Robinson shouted down to the men and women on the sands. With a flurry of movement, the crowd surrounded the carriage to push it into the sea. The icy North Sea shocked the launchers but they stuck to their task and gradually, when they were waist deep, the *Harbinger* floated. The crew pulled on their oars and the boat made headway into the waves.

"Heave, men, heave," shouted John Robinson. He peered into the snow and sleet, dashed into his face by the fierce gale. "Pull towards Auburn. There's a brig aground."

The slender boat carved its way through the breaking rollers and eventually reached the relative safety of the unbroken sea. Although the crew were not regular crew members they hauled on their oars with determination. David Purdon glanced across at John Clappison and the men shared a nervous smile. For both men this work was far more strenuous than they had experienced before.

Despite their weatherproof sou'westers, capes, leggings and boots they were already soaked to the skin. David Purdon looked down at his hands and saw blood seeping between his fingers. "I'll not be making toy boats for young James for a few days," he thought, as he gazed at his bleeding hands. But he gripped the oar even tighter and heaved for all he was worth.

The *Harbinger* gradually closed the distance to the brig grounded on the shelving sands of Bridlington's south bay. On this part of the coast, the water was shallow for a long way out, as shown by curling breaking waves in the distance. Boats which came aground here were still a long way from safety, hundreds of yards from the grassy dunes. The brig, *Delta,* was stuck fast. Huge waves thundered into her stern and were gradually turning her broadside. Once she was broadside, it would be a matter of only minutes before the tide smashed her to pieces.

The *Harbinger* crawled closer. John Robinson cupped his hands and hollered: "Ahoy, *Delta!*"

A bundle of cloth fast in the rigging became a man waving to the lifeboat. "Help! Help!" came a call in a voice wavering with exhaustion.

"Come on, men. Heave!" John Robinson encouraged more effort and *Harbinger* closed on the *Delta.* The tide careened off the side of the *Delta* straight into the path of the *Harbinger.* John Robinson brought her bow to head into these waves and the gap between the boats narrowed.

The men in the *Harbinger* gazed up at the man in the rigging and shouted: "Jump! Jump, while you have the chance!"

The man in the rigging waved again. "I can't! I'm scared!"

"Come on, jump! Jump!" The last word was screamed by the crew. The man on the *Delta* seemed to make his decision.

But John Robinson had to pull the *Harbinger* away from the *Delta* to take up a better position. Encouraging his crew again, Robinson brought the lifeboat close to the *Delta* again. The crew shouted "Jump! Jump!" again to the man in the rigging, and he prepared to leap.

But he hesitated as he pointed beyond the *Harbinger.* "Look out!" he shouted.

The lifeboat crew turned and watched as a huge wave bore down on them. It lifted the *Harbinger* then dropped her into the trough that followed.

"Hang on!" Jim Robinson shouted. Dick Purdon and John Clappison exchanged glances, their eyes filled with fear.

The wave hit the side of the *Delta*, and rebounded into the *Harbinger*'s bow. The bow lifted but the stern of the boat dropped into the trough of another wave. In seconds the boat was pointing to the racing clouds. With a huge splash she dropped back into the waves on her side, spilling out all nine men.

Another huge wave charged down on the *Delta*, smashing into the woodwork, and carrying away the rigging with the unfortunate man who would not jump.

In the boiling seas, men floundered and gasped. Coxswain Robinson managed to grab the lifeboat, now upside down in the water. He held on to the ropes and looked for his crewmates. He threw his scarf out to crewman Robert Hopper bobbing up and down near him and hauled him to the side of the boat.

Another wave, larger than those before, bore down on the lifeboat, flinging it over to float on the waves. Richard Bedlington had been under the boat and was now inside. He reached over and helped the other two men aboard. All three peered into the storm to find their crewmates. A man surfaced close by, reaching for the lifeboat. The three in the boat heard him shout "Help!" but he was swallowed by another wave. Those in the lifeboat saw despair in his eyes as he disappeared from sight.

The *Delta* turned broadside to the oncoming waves and within minutes she was pounded to matchwood. The *Harbinger*, riding atop the waves, was carried down the coast until she came aground at Wilsthorpe, a mile south of the harbour. Without oars, the three men in the lifeboat were unable to do a thing.

Chapter 6

10 February 1871

Along the sea wall, north of the harbour, onlookers watched with alarm at the sights before them. A group of men and women dashed into the water, linked hands and made a human chain. With the waves surging past them, they stood chest-deep in water, the spray splashing into their faces. The doomed boats came nearer and the crews peered over the sides of their boats to see their rescuers.

"Here, matey. Give us your hand. We'll pass you to safety," came a call. The sailor, eyes full of fear, clambered over the side of the vessel, and lowered himself on a rope until he was in the water. He grabbed the first hand offered and was passed down the line to the safety of the shore. Another man swung over the side of the boat as a wave smashed into it. His grip on the rope relaxed and he fell fifteen feet into the waves. The men in the line grabbed him, lifted him upright, and he too was passed along the line to the sand.

On the cliff top, men with a rocket apparatus attempted to send a line over to the ships. But the fury of the gale flung the rope back at them. They tried several times but it was hopeless. They collected their equipment and went down to the harbour where they hoped they would be more effective.

The hulks of beached ships were swept by huge waves, grinding and pounding the vessels to kindling. On the *Margaret*, of Ipswich, a man clung to the wheel. The remainder of the crew had already attempted to launch a small boat but it capsized the instant it hit the water. The men floundered in the waves but all were lost.

The lone man hung on for over an hour, then, cold and exhausted, he fell overboard and was drowned.

Men struggled through the shallows to find a place on

the beach on which to fall. Gasping and aching, they lay for some minutes before they heard kindly words from one of the townswomen.

"Here, sailor. Have a drink." The sailor wrapped his hands around a mug of tea, which he sipped. "Thanks, missus," was all he could say. And when he was led away up the road to the cliff top, it was all he could do to walk.

Rev. Lloyd Graeme, of Sewerby House, strode up and down the sands on the north side, offering comfort where he could. He knew that what these men wanted was a warm meal and a dry bed. His shout could be heard all morning through the disaster. "Here's another one, ladies. Get him home. Make sure he wants for nothing." And another home welcomed an extra guest for a couple of days.

Nothing was denied the shipwrecked. Kindness flowed everywhere. Feuds were forgotten as townspeople realised that they were facing something much bigger than their own bitter rivalries.

At the harbour, things were no better. Ship after ship attempted to reach the calm waters of the harbour, but one by one they failed. The *Agnes May*, of London, tried to squeeze through the harbour entrance but a rogue wave smashed her into the stone. The backwash lifted her outside the harbour wall and she scraped down the south pier until she was pounded to grief at the cliffs.

Another boat came towards the entrance. Onlookers screamed encouragement at the crew. "Hang on! Hang on!" But the power of the wind and the fury of the waves flung the men from the frail security of their ship into the seas. The onlookers could see the eyes of the dying men as they floundered in the sea, an arm's length away. Many local men and women spent the day in tears as they watched the drama.

Women bustled and hurried everywhere. They took rescued men to their homes or the cafés on the sea front. The public houses were soon filled with distraught seamen, concerned for their shipmates.

Among the many men struggling to save lives was Kit Brown, who, warmed and rested, threw his rope into the waves many many times. He dragged man after man out of the water, to send them home with Mary. Despite having crewed the lifeboat for several hours, Kit was unable to ignore the suffering of everyone involved. He watched in amazement as wives of the lifeboat crew waded armpit deep to help distressed sailors ashore.

As the tide receded, piles of timber, sails and ropes began to accumulate at the foot of the seawalls. In some places it was as much as nine feet deep. Although ships were still running aground, local womenfolk started hunting through the wood and sails for anyone they'd missed.

Mary found Kit in the tumult and threw her arms round him. "Oh, Kit. It's terrible, terrible!"

They clung to each other. "Aye, lass. I hope we never see anything like this again."

Chapter 7

12 February 1871

Kit Brown woke to a cacophony of gulls as the nightmare wave swept over him again. He allowed himself a moment of calm, before stretching his legs to ease their ache. He flexed his arms and then made fists of his fingers, feeling the agony of his torn palms.

He listened to the gulls as they wheeled and soared over the harbour. He could also hear the splashing of waves and the clatter of ropes and rigging on the moored cobles.

There was only a little light in the bedroom so Kit knew it was before dawn. He visualised the sun breaking away from the horizon over the Bay.

Then he shuddered as his mind replayed those waves again and again. Huge and green they bore down on him as if the very devil was riding them. He remembered clinging to the oar with both hands as the water flung itself at him. The waves swept over him and his hands were torn away from the oar.

Kit shuddered again and clung to the blanket covering him. He was cold. He closed his eyes and the wave was there again, towering over him, its top edge a flurry of spray, its body solid water moving without pause to crash over him.

Kit looked at the sea in his mind's eye and realised he could never look at it in the same way again. All his life he had made his living on the sea. At times he loved it, loved its moods, its whims, its awkwardnesses. But, he realised, after the *Harbinger* capsized, fear of the sea had come into his mind. Now he was uneasy because he felt the sea would be seeking revenge for his audacity.

Kit turned onto his back and gazed at the ceiling. He thought of his life at sea. As a boy of fourteen he'd sailed with his uncle Christofer Brown in the *Westminster*, a four-masted barque, one of the finest ships afloat at that time. There had been trouble with his uncle and aunt, who had accompanied her husband. When in Bombay, Kit had left the boat and joined *Rose*, a sailing brig bound for Holland. But the boat hit rocks in a gale and he and another sailor found themselves on the Dutch shore. A farmer found them and took them to his home. He didn't report his discovery and Kit and his friend were made to work on the farm for months until they escaped. They made their way to Amsterdam where they persuaded a captain to take them back to England.

Kit smiled to himself as he remembered the rejoicing when he turned up in Bridlington.

Kit reflected too on his ancestors, all of them connected with the sea. He remembered how his father, who was on the *Isabella*, a barque-rigged ship, found the explorer Sir John Ross on the Arctic icecap and brought him home. Ross's Polar Expedition had been missing, causing anxiety in England.

Outside Kit's cottage the gulls squawked and screeched, and his mind came back to the present.

He turned on to his side and put an arm over Mary. She murmured as she woke and Kit moved closer. He reached round, cupped a breast and wondered what Mary would call their next child.

Chapter 8

12 February 1871

"Terrible sight, Mr Brown." Captain George Symons pointed to the men and women of Bridlington searching the debris along the sea wall.

"It surely is, Captain." Kit Brown leaned on the railings outside Symons' home on Cliff Terrace overlooking the harbour.

"You know, when I was watching the storm on Friday I couldn't believe what I saw." George Symons gazed out at the sea.

"What do you mean?" Kit Brown asked.

"Well, the fact that nearly everyone from the Quay was out there on the beach, helping launch the lifeboats, helping the crews and the rescued when they came back." George paused. "All those men who went out in the lifeboats. I don't know how they do it."

"Do what?" Kit Brown turned to look at the Captain.

"Go out in seas like that. It must have been terribly dangerous. But still they went. I don't think I could do that."

"That's odd coming from someone like you," said Kit.

"Someone like me?" asked the Captain.

"Yes, you. A VC winner. That makes you someone special," Kit suggested.

"No, not really. I was only doing what I had to do."

Kit was quick to reply. "But that's what we say: 'We're only doing our job'."

"But," said the Captain, "you and your men didn't get paid for what you did. Oh, I know you get a small reward afterwards, but that's not the same as being paid to do it. No-one can command you to do what you did. In the Army, people are commanded to do this, do that, or the other. And we have to do it, even if it means looking down the barrel of a gun." George Symons shuddered at his memories of the Crimea.

"There's no way I could do that," Kit offered. "When I'm at sea I have some control of what's happening. That's not so in war, is it?"

"I'm sure of one thing. There's no way you could get me in a boat to face those seas. That's really heroic. I think you all deserve medals for what you do." George Symons looked back at the sea.

"Medals? You don't expect to get medals when you're out there. You're trying to save lives. I love the sea, but if I can prevent it, she'll not take any lives while I'm there." Kit's face looked determined, and he seemed to speak to the waves and tide.

"Well, I suppose one day we'll both understand what real heroism is, Brown." George Symons touched the brim of his hat and went up the steps to his front door.

"Perhaps," thought Kit Brown, "One day we will know what makes a hero."

Chapter 9

12 February 1871

Mary Brown's numbed fingers reached for another limpet. She was weary and cold. Her basket was heavy, half-filled as it was with the bait destined for Kit Brown's lines.

For nearly two hours Mary stood on wet sand reaching and cutting the shellfish from the harbour walls. The rocks on which she stood were treacherous with seaweed, and a slip would have meant another bruise, another graze. Perhaps even an unwanted plunge into a rockpool.

Mary wore a black knitted shawl over her shoulders, one of her husband's cast-off shirts, a long dark brown skirt, thick black stockings and lace-up boots. Even though it was mid-day, it was cold at the base of the pier. In this corner between the pier and the road above, the crashing waters of high tide threw spray over the houses close by. At low tide, it was a meeting place for the fisherwives, flithering for bait.

"Are you off for some coal later, Mary?" Betsy Purvis stopped her work to break the silence.

"Aye, I am." Mary Brown turned and breathed a deep sigh. "And I shall be looking out for sailors too."

Both women bent to their tasks in silence.

"How's Dick? Kit said he was injured," Mary said eventually, her face showing concern.

"Well, he slipped when he was hanging onto a rope and scraped his shin. He says it's painful, but he reckons it'll mend."

"I'm so glad Kit wasn't on board when . . ." Mary stopped, tears glinting in her eyes.

"Aye, and Dick. I don't know how I'd be if I lost him."

"It must be awful to lose your man like that. I don't know how those women cope. Look at poor James' wife.

Carried off to an asylum in York, they say. Poor woman Good job they had no kids."

Both women fell silent again and started to hack at limpets with their knives.

"Here, Betsy, look at this!" Mary Brown held out her palm.

Betsy Purvis put her bag on the sand. Pieces of coal spilled out to join the flotsam and jetsam on Bridlington's north beach.

"What have you got, Mary?" she asked, approaching her friend.

"A cross. A wooden cross. It's really nice. Some poor wretch has lost it," replied Mary.

"Aye. Along with his life probably, poor soul."

"I'll give it to the vicar when we've done here."

Mary and Betsy turned back to the beach. All along the seawall the two women could see piles of wood, cloth, sails, rope and broken oars. In some places they had to look up to see the tops of the piles.

There was such a quantity of coal and timber on the beach that the authorities had given permission for local men and women to take away what they wanted.

Mary and Betsy bent to collect the coal. Already busy were scores of boys and girls given the day off school to help clear the beach of coal.

Spars and deck timbers were hauled up the steps to the road where horse-drawn carts carried away the spoils.

Fishermen in dark blue ganseys pulled lengths of rope from the wreckage. If they were still of use, these were coiled and left at the foot of the steps to be spliced.

Clothing was turned over and over as the women sought a name, anything, to provide identification of the scores of seamen drowned two days before.

Mary and Betsy heaved at a large sail and stepped back in horror at the corpse beneath. Its ashen face stared at them with blank eyes and Betsy turned to Mary: "Cover him up, Mary, and I'll go and find the priest."

Betsy hurried away as fast as she could through the piles of wreckage.

Mary took off her shawl and covered the man's head. She looked down his body and saw a rosary protruding from a pocket. She took the cross from her apron and realised it was made of the same wood as the beads.

Mary reached down to place the cross with the beads.

"You need this cross more than I do, sailor," Mary said, adding "God be with you."

Mary turned her back on the body and faced the sea, so calm, so different from the recent tumult.

The sun shone from a sharp February day and glinted from Mary's tears.

Chapter 10

14 February 1871

The procession of mourners was over half a mile long. Blinds were drawn, flags fluttered at half mast, and the pavements were deep with onlookers. Since dawn hundreds of travellers had arrived in the town. Local societies were also represented: the Chief Lord of the Feoffees, the committee of the Sailors' and Workingmen's Club, the Amicable Society, as well as members of the shipping fraternity from Hull and elsewhere. And at the end of the procession, the bodies of local lifeboatmen and other seamen.

The small group of men huddled round the door of Priory Church. They had walked the length of the outside wall, across the width at the east end and back along the northern side. At the west door, open for this special day, they hesitated.

"By heck, Kit. It's a bit bigger than Sailors' Bethel," Dick Purvis whispered.

"Aye, lad, and a deal more grand, too," Kit peered round the edge of the door into the depths of the church. Sunlight blazed through the east window, sweeping a kaleidoscope of colour through the nave.

"Are we off in, then?" Richard Bedlington asked, straightening his jacket collar.

The men were hesitant, and moved from foot to foot, unsure of what to do next.

"Look," said Kit, "there's Rev. Blakeney. We'd best go in."

The men shuffled through the door into the cool of the church. They walked down the aisle, and looked at each other when they realised every eye was on them. Kit raised his eyebrows in question, and Dick hunched his shoulders a little to express his lack of understanding. They reached the front pews and filed into the spaces left for them.

The organist started to play and the congregation stood.

Kit Brown picked up a hymn book and thumbed through the pages until he found what he was looking for. He pushed the book towards Dick and both men looked at the words.

The hymn was unfamiliar to them. The fishermen were more accustomed to the Methodist hymns of the Sailors' Bethel, tucked away a few feet from the water's edge on the south side of the harbour.

As the sound of the organ died, Rev. Blakeney strode to the pulpit steps, and climbed them until he was gazing down at the congregation.

Kit's attention wandered as he gazed around the church, marvelling at the stained glass windows, the high arches and the shaped stones. And then his mind went back to the day when his six comrades lost their battle with the sea.

It had been a pleasant spring day on the ninth of February, but at three o'clock that Friday morning, the tenth, clouds became darker and there was unmistakable evidence of a change in the weather. An hour later, the wind rose and veered towards the south-east. With abrupt suddenness, a storm rose up increasing in violence until it became a hurricane. Snow and sleet were driven so hard it was nearly impossible to see.

The ships anchored in the bay were in a precarious situation. They were now on a lee-shore and in the teeth of a gale. By six o'clock, the wind moved to the east-south-east, still accompanied by sleet and snow.

By dawn the ships were in great danger. In these conditions, mariners usually kept well away from the coast. But the armada of ships in Bridlington Bay were unable to leave its shallows for the depths of the North

Sea. They were on the wrong side of Smithwick Sands, and the storm threw huge breaking waves over the shallows. And the captains were unable to sail either back towards Flamborough Head or southerly towards the Holderness coast to sail round Smithwick. They were trapped.

Townspeople recognised the danger and ran to the seawall. There they watched the ships attempting to reach harbour through a blinding snow storm. By seven o'clock the rocket apparatus was prepared for the expected emergencies.

A south-country barge failed to make harbour and was driven into the wall of the Esplanade. The crew took to the rigging as the seas broke over them and their vessel. The rocket apparatus, manned by five men of the coastguard, failed in its attempt to get a line to the boat. The crew was one of the first to be rescued by the RNLI lifeboat *Robert Whitworth*.

Within the next few hours, many ships ran for the beach on the north side of the harbour, but all came ashore on the south side on the powerful tide. In this area of the bay, the sea was shallower than at the north, and ships grounded much farther out. The lifeboats had much farther to sail to make a rescue and huge waves and a snowstorm still hampered the crews.

On the north side, skippers drove their boats towards the sands, and in some cases their crews were able to wade to shore because they were much closer to the beach. Local men and women made human chains through the pounding surf so that rescued sailors could make their way ashore.

A collier went ashore near Sewerby, two miles north of the harbour, her bottom smashed out by the rocks. The crew were rescued by coastguards wading up to their armpits in the waves. The men were rewarded with cheers from the spectators on the sands.

Kit's mind caught the word "peril" and he left his

thoughts. This hymn he knew. He joined his colleagues and the congregation in *Eternal Father*. Tears pricked his eyes and there was of a catch in his voice as he tried to sing: "Oh hear us when we cry to Thee, for those in peril on the sea."

For those in peril on the sea, Kit thought. He took a deep breath and wiped his eyes.

Chapter 11

22 February 1871

Kit Brown gazed at the placid sea in Bridlington Bay as he ran his right hand through his tight beard. Once again, he realised he didn't understand the sea. Yesterday, it was in tumult, today it was benign. But that was the sea, thought Kit. That was why towns like Bridlington had a lifeboat. And why men like him had to hazard their lives to save others. Any why six of his friends lost their lives.

Kit's gaze swept over the north beach where the remnants of two brigantines moved gracefully through the wavelets on the beach. Among the wreckage above high-water mark, Kit could make out several figures dressed in black. Among them was his wife Mary, collecting coal, cast ashore as the wrecked vessels were pounded by the previous day's gales.

Kit dragged a lungful of pure spring air, turned away from the sea and walked towards the Sailors' and Workingmen's Club on Cliff Street.

As he turned the corner, he saw the back of Dick Purvis, his fellow lifeboatman. And coming towards him, limped the squat shape of Captain Atkin, the lifeboat secretary.

Kit lengthened his stride as he formed his arguments against the secretary for the debacle of twelve days ago.

In the workingmen's club, voices were raised and occasionally a shout could be heard over the hubbub. The room was hazy with smoke, the pungent fumes of cheap tobacco swirling as doors were opened and closed.

Kit Brown nodded his greeting to Dick Purvis as the two men entered the room.

"Hey up, Dick lad. Thou all right?"

"Aye, Kit. Thanks. My back's bloody sore where I got clobbered by an oar, and my shin's still red raw."

"Well, lad, I hope them committee men are going to take notice of us at last. It was a complete farce from start to finish."

Ribald shouts and boos greeted Captain Atkin as he climbed the few steps to the dais. He stopped on each step and his face was pink with exertion.

He made his way to the centre of the stage, shouting for attention and waving his walking stick.

"It's all right for you Atkin. You weren't out there!" The voice held a touch of bitterness as it boomed from the throng.

"Aye, and unless you listen to us, it'll happen again." This response was greeted with shouts of "Aye!" and sporadic applause.

"Now, lads, we're all here to see what happened and how to prevent it happening again." Atkin pointed his stick at the row of men with dark suits and solemn faces.

One by one, the men stood as Captain Atkin called out their names. "We have Mr Postill. You know him. He's the one who started this workingmen's club through the kindness of his heart."

There was a smattering of polite applause, but also mutterings of "Get on with it, Atkin!"

"Next we have the Rev. Lloyd-Graeme. He's helped us with lifeboat funding in the past and I'm sure we can count on him again."

Captain Atkin let his gaze roam round the room, finally coming to rest on Kit Brown.

"And we also have Captain Ward from the National Lifeboat Institution. He has come to tell us what the Institution has to say."

Suddenly the murmurings in the room increased to mutterings then a shout of "To hell with the Institution" rang from the back of the hall.

"Now then, lads, you'll all have a chance if you want to say something."

Captain Atkin nodded to Rev. Graeme who stood up and motioned for the men to be silent.

"Gentlemen. We cannot but be hurt by what happened recently. Our colleagues gave their all for their fellow man, and no-one can do more than that. What we must do now, is look forward. We must discover what went wrong and how we can make sure it never happens again."

The hardened faces of the men, sharpened by wild east winds and freezing spray, turned to their fellow sailors and nodded approval.

"You all feel your loss greatly and know that, but for the grace of Our Lord God, it could have been any one of you. I know that some of you were resting when the boat was lost, but you must not feel guilty. You had done your bit. It was the turn of others. They were lost but it was not your fault.

"Others of you will be feeling that you should have been on that last fateful trip. But that, too, is wrong. It was pure chance who was on the boat at that time.

"You were able to show your grief at the funeral at the Priory. Here, please keep grief and emotion in check so that we can help to make Bridlington Bay a safer place for all, and that includes you men. You are the men who crew the lifeboats. You are the men on whom others rely. You are the saviours of mariners at sea as Our Lord is the saviour of our souls."

Throughout the room, the words of Rev. Graeme had calmed the men. They looked at each other, nodding and agreeing with his sentiments.

Captain Atkin said: "Thank you Rev. Graeme. Now I'd like to ask for a comment by our good friend Mr Postill."

Mr Postill, a short man bulging out of his trousers and jacket, took a sip of water before standing. He leaned forward, his fingers spread on the table. He looked round the room, his eyes catching the glance of nearly every man.

"We lost some good men that day and we're all sorry it happened. David Purdon was a great credit to the town, especially as he didn't have to volunteer. He gallantly took Dick's place," and he pointed to Dick Purvis, "after he'd been out seven times. James Watson was a member of this club and his name will be for ever connected with the bravery of the men of Bridlington lifeboat.

"The other men, Robert Pickering, William Cobb, John Clappison and Richard Atkin, were our friends and colleagues. We worked with each other, we spent time together in the reading room, or enjoying a pint in the *Coble & Anchor* in Burlington Quay.

"We are grateful for the lives of Richard Bedlington, Robert Hopper and John Robinson.

"None of us wanted that disaster. And surely none of you hold the committee responsible in any way."

A bitter voice shouted: "Maybe not, Postill, but you lot were in charge."

"Gentlemen, gentlemen. Let's not be too quick to apportion blame. There must be something we can learn from this incident."

"Ask the Institution to give us a surf boat. A proper boat." Harry Hutchinson stood up to make his point. "Men from the Quay know what's best for this bay. What I don't want is another heavy beast like that thing the Institution gave us."

"Yes, yes, Harry. We know the feelings of the men on that score, and the decision on the next boat will come soon."

Captain Atkin limped to the centre of the stage, and gestured that Postill sit down. Postill glanced at the men at his side of the table for support but they were staring straight into the crowd of fishermen. He lowered himself into his chair.

"We're very lucky today," started Captain Atkin, "that we have with us Captain Ward of the Institution. They provided us with the national boat, *Robert Whitworth*. If it wasn't for them we'd only have the fishermen's boat, the *Harbinger*."

"Aye, and it was a bloody good job we had the *Harbinger* last Friday," shouted Kit Brown. "God only knows what would have happened if we hadn't had her.

48

And God knows what would have happened to those men at sea."

"Please, gentlemen, let Captain Ward have his say."

Resplendent in his finely cut uniform, white shirt and shining shoes, Captain Ward strode to the centre of the stage. He stiffened his back, glanced at Kit Brown, and began: "Gentlemen. Thank you for attending today. I know you are all angry at the loss of life a week last Friday. So is the Institution. We are, just as you are, sorry that this disaster happened. But sometimes events are out of our control. On this occasion, despite the valiant efforts of our crews, lives were lost. You are sorrowing for your family members, relatives and colleagues, while up and down the country other families are mourning their loss. It is not easy being in the lifeboat service. Whatever we do, we seem to be wrong. Despite the fact that the *Robert Whitworth* was the best design of boat to date, she proved too heavy and managed only three trips. She did save lives, however, four off the brigantine *Friends Increase*, six off the brig *Echo* and six more off the brig *Windsor*. That's sixteen lives saved."

"Aye, but *Harbinger* saved more and she would have gone out again and again if she hadn't been lost. You can't blame us for what happened!" There was anger in the voice.

"The *Harbinger* was a fine boat . . ." someone in the audience called.

"But she wasn't a self-righter," interrupted Capt Ward. "If she had been a self-righter the disaster would have been averted. That's why we have to have self-righting boats in our service."

Another man shouted: "Maybe, but not when they're too heavy to row. It was back-breaking in that thing. Look at my hands. Hardly a scrap of flesh left on them. It were too heavy, far too heavy."

Captain Ward stalked along the stage in front of the table, the eyes of Captain Atkin, Mr Postill and Rev. Graeme following him.

"You see, men, the Institution has to have a boat that protects the lives of its crew. We have to look after our men as well as those who are shipwrecked."

Once again there was a shout from the crowd: "But you're not looking after the men or the shipwrecked if the boat's too damn heavy!"

The air in the room grew warmer as men jostled to make themselves heard. The smoke wreathed round the gas mantles and eddied round the small windows of the club.

Kit Brown watched the wisps as they disappeared and his mind went back to the day before the disaster as he walked slowly along the beach at Bridlington.

The day had dawned bright and clear. The sea was flat calm and Kit counted the barques, brigs, brigantines and snows at anchor along the horizon.

He reached 30 and realised that there were at least twice that number. He knew the ships were laden to the gunnels with all manner of material: coal, stone, wood, cement. In the calm of that morning, captains had dropped anchor as they waited for a breeze.

Kit had learned that many had left port at Newcastle or Middlesbrough bound for London with coal for Paris, where the Germans held the city in seige.

Kit ran down the harbour steps and walked briskly to Crane Wharf. There he jumped aboard a rowing boat, and rowed it along the harbour wall until he reached a slipway where he tied the boat to a coble. He leapt onto the quay and took one of a stand of barrels near a water pump at the side of the sloping roadway.

He rolled one of the barrels to the pump and started to fill it with water. When it was half full, Kit gripped the top and turned it along its bottom edge back to the coble. Using a small gallows winch he lowered the barrel into the bottom of the boat.

He filled four more barrels and eventually had them secured.

Kit paused for breath and mopped his brow with his neckerchief. He tied it round his throat and looked up the roadway. He smiled. "Right on time, Dick." Dick Purvis jumped into the boat and slapped Kit on the shoulder.

"Grand day, Kit," Dick said.

"Let's hope it lasts. I've a few jobs to get done provided it stays fine."

"Are we taking water out today, Kit?" Dick gestured at the barrels of water.

"Aye, thought that lot out there could do with some. They've been there a day and a night now. It might be a couple of days before there's a breeze."

"OK, Kit. Let's go!"

The coble was soon scudding across the waters of the Bay. The bow wave curled into a brief white strip of lace across the blue of sea. The only sounds were the flapping of the sail, and the splash of water along the side of the boat. Kit's hand on the tiller was still, the wind pushing the coble towards the Smithwick Sands.

This huge sandbank lay across the Bay like a dormant serpent, unseen during the calm and well below the keel of Kit's coble.

Kit chose a brigantine, the *Flower of May*, and with casual skill brought the coble alongside.

Kit cupped his hands and shouted: "Ahoy, *Flower of May*. Ahoy." A dozen heads peered over the side of the brigantine.

"Ahoy," came a return shout. "What do you want?"

"It's Brown out of Bridlington. Are you needing water?"

"Aye, lad. That we do. I'm skipper Martinson. How much have you got?"

Kit kept the coble alongside the brigantine as the waves pushed between them. "Five barrels half full. What you got?"

"Coal."

"Coal?" Kit asked.

"Aye. Do you want some?"

51

"Have you nothing better? Rum, or whisky?"

"Nay, lad, not this trip. But you're welcome to a bag of coal in exchange for a barrel of water." The skipper pointed along the side of his ship to a pair of seamen lowering a rope.

"Okay," Kit shouted, and allowed the tide to push the coble towards the rope.

He tied the rope to a barrel of water, and yelled, "Haul away!" He guided the barrel until it left his reach and watched it disappear over the gunwhales of the larger ship.

Within a couple of minutes, a sack was lowered into the coble, and Dick hauled it to the stern. Kit tied the rope to another barrel and this too went into the brigantine.

Everyone worked in harmony and twenty minutes later Kit was at tiller as the coble sped back to harbour.

"Nice exchange there, Kit," said Dick, rubbing his hands to ease the pain in his fingers.

"Aye, not bad. You'll take one, I reckon?" Kit pointed to a sack of coal.

"Thanks, Kit, that I will. Betsy will be glad of that come winter. What about the rest?"

"Well," said Kit, "Our Jess can have one. He's worse off than we are at present. He'll maybe sell some and keep some. And as for the others, well they'll keep till back end."

As the discussion about the destination of the coal progressed, the grey stone of Bridlington harbour was getting closer. The vessel approached the harbour mouth, and the talking ceased as both men worked the boat.

Across the harbour mouth, the small sandbank caused its usual chaotic seas and only Kit's sure hand on the tiller and Dick's lowering the sail at the right moment brought the vessel through easily.

The coble was tied up again at Crane Wharf and both Kit and Dick hauled a sack from the boat on to the steps. Once on the steps, the men hoisted the sacks on to their shoulders and walked the few yards to Kit's cottage.

Kit dropped his sack and Dick carried on walking. He turned and asked: "Do you want a hand with the others?"

"No, Dick. You're OK. Our Jess will give us a hand. If he wants a sack he can carry it." Kit laughed and left Dick as he returned to the boat.

A shout of "What do you think, Kit?" brought Kit back to the present.

He remembered hearing the words 'lifeboats,' 'surf,' 'the Institution,' and 'life-saving,' so he said: "What do I think? Well, I reckon as how we need a surf boat. One that rides over the waves and not through them. It needs a flatter bottom than the National boats and if it's the right shape it'll not need to be a self-righter." He noticed Mr Ward about to get to his feet, and he carried on: "No, Mr Ward. It needn't be a self-righter. The very things that make your boat a self-righter helps it turn over in the first place. Great slab-sided things they are. A big sea can take them straight over. Granted they turn back right side up, but there always a chance you'll lose the crew. Now a surf boat will just rise over the waves and because it's lower in the water it'll have less side to the wind. So, a well-built light boat is just what we need."

There were shouts of approval from the massed sailors, but an occasional call of dissent.

A voice shouted: "I agree with Kit. I was in the National boat and it was too heavy. It took all our strength to do just three trips."

"Aye," shouted another voice, "the *Harbinger* went out seven times. She could have kept going out but we lost her. And that wasn't down to the fact she wasn't a self-righter. The National boat would have gone over in those seas."

"Look, Postill. We're the men who crew the lifeboats. Why doesn't the Institution listen to us." An angry voice quietened the chatter. "We know what's best for these waters. Bridlington Bay is shallow. It's no more than six fathoms deep right until you get to Smithwick Sands. So there's a lot of surf."

Dick Purvis walked to the front of the crowd and called up to the men at the table. "And it's the surf that's the problem for the boats. If you don't get into the unbroken water quickly, the boats are swamped. The *Harbinger* was the right boat at the right time. Pity we lost her."

He turned to the crowded room, and shouted: "Give us the right boat and we'll do the job."

There was a cry of "Aye" from the floor as the men stamped their feet in agreement.

Captain Atkin gestured for quiet: "Right, men. Listen. I propose that this Sailors' & Workingmen's Club take the *Harbinger* into its ownership. Instead of it being just the fishermen's boat it becomes the Club boat. That way we can provide funds for its repair and so on."

The men in the room looked at each other and nodded. After a vote had been taken, and every man agreed, Mr Postill stood up.

"Gentlemen. As you all know, Count Batthyany paid for the *Harbinger*. I have heard today that if *we* take on the boat and get her repaired he will provide a carriage at his expense. I think we should agree to accept the Count's generous offer."

Kit and Dick looked at each other and smiled. Kit said, "Perhaps the lifeboat service in Bridlington is going to get better after all."

Chapter 12

26 May 1871

"Things could have been a lot better, that we must agree."
Captain Ward, of the National Lifeboat Institution, gazed
at the group of fishermen before him.

The men were assembled in the large meeting room in
the Sailors' and Workingmen's Club. They had been
called to consider the next steps in the improvement of the
lifeboat service.

"We do need to take into account the concerns of local
men when we are installing a lifeboat. It's obvious that
they know their own waters better than anyone else.
However, and this is where the difficulty lies, the
Institution wishes to design life-saving boats which will
serve many communities and not have to design boats for
particular harbours or coastlines."

He looked at the faces of the men in the crowd. Honest,
hard-working men who put their lives on the line every
time the lifeboat was launched. He was torn between
what he must say on behalf of the Institution and his
feelings for those who had lost six of their comrades.

"When I return to the Institution, I will state, quite
categorically, that the men of Bridlington wish to be
supplied with a boat to their requirements. A surf boat,
one that will meet with their approval."

With the cheers of the men, Captain Ward sat down. He
glanced across at Mr Postill, who nodded agreement, and
then noticed the Rev. Graeme's broad smile. Captain
Atkin's face was expressionless as he stood up and
addressed the meeting.

"You men have heard the arguments for and against
various types of boat. Some of you want the town to have
a surf boat." He paused to allow the cheers to die down.
"Others of you," and he looked particularly at a few men

who had been vociferous during the meeting, "feel that the Institution must decide which boats be allocated. While the Institution favours self-righting vessels as a policy, they must not be allowed to overlook the wishes of the men who man those boats. Captain Ward will make his recommendations to his committee on his return to his office. So, gentlemen, that concludes this meeting. Good night."

Captain Atkin turned away from the crowd and shook hands with those behind the table as he walked down the stage. After shaking hands with the Captain, the men shook hands with each other and walked off.

"What do you think, Kit? Will they let us have a surf boat?" Dick Purvis grabbed Kit Brown's arm as they filed outside.

"Don't know, Dick. That Captain Ward speaks well, but he is an Institution man. He'll find it difficult to persuade those who make the decisions. But we can hope."

A fisherman in front of Kit turned and said: "What right has the Institution to tell us what sort of boat to have? Surely we can raise the money for a private boat. The Count bought us *Harbinger*. Perhaps he could be persuaded to buy another boat."

"I don't know about that," said Kit. "He's given us a carriage for *Harbinger*. There's a lot of brass needed to pay for a lifeboat. Why, *Harbinger* cost him over three hundred pounds. That's a fortune!"

"Aye," agreed Dick. "I doubt if he'd want to do that again. But I hope somebody can find the money. We need a better boat."

Chapter 13

26 December 1871

Aboard the new lifeboat, Kit Brown and Dick Purvis gasped when they saw the size of the crowd on the beach. All along the foreshore, thousands of people had massed to see the new lifeboat, despite the overcast blustery day.

The lifeboat, its coat of white paint gleaming, started its day at ten o'clock that Boxing Day morning with crew members aboard. She'd left the new boathouse, a further gift from the Rev. Lloyd-Graeme of Sewerby House, and proceeded up Quay Road to the green opposite Priory Church.

There, in High Green Dyke, she had been launched, her first taste of water. The crew had taken the oars and demonstrated their skills to the watching hundreds.

Her baptism over, she was recarriaged and dragged by six horses along the road to Marton Hall, and then to Sewerby House. At twelve noon, Kit, Dick and the other crew members listened to Rev. Mark Tyler, vicar of St John the Evangelist at Sewerby: "May Almighty God bless this boat and may it be the means of saving life."

Then Rev. Yarborough Lloyd-Graeme, who had paid for the boat, stepped forward.

"It gives me great pleasure to introduce my daughter Emily, who will officially christen this vessel."

Emily, her delicate teenage frame swathed in a fine white dress, held a glass of wine over the bow of the boat and said: "This lifeboat I name *Seagull*. May she sail over the waves with the grace of her namesake." She then poured the wine over the boat amid cheering from the crowd.

Rev. Lloyd-Graeme then said, "This is a day of great importance to the people of Bridlington. We are gathered to christen our new lifeboat. As we remember all too well, in that dreadful storm of February last, the *Harbinger* was too small to be completely effective as a lifeboat. The *Seagull* is designed and built to the requirements of our men, local men, who manage and crew her. The National boat was too large and unwieldy, and although the principle of self-righting is a good one it is not appropriate for the waters of Bridlington Bay. The Institution is unwilling to take on this boat as it is not to their design, but I am delighted to hand over the *Seagull* into the care of the Sailors' and Workingmen's Club at the Quay in Bridlington. Let us hope that the *Seagull*, should she ever be wanted, rides in safety over the ocean waves and be the means of saving many lives."

Kit and Dick applauded as the speech ended, and within a few moments there were cheers and shouts of approval from the whole crowd.

The horses were brought back to be shackled to the carriage, and the *Seagull* was hauled away from Sewerby House.

"Well, Dick, what's tha think?" Kit waved to the people on the packed pavements.

"I've seen nowt like it, Kit. They seem to be in favour of *Seagull*. Let's hope she's a good boat and does us proud."

"She'll be all right. Once we get a few things into shape. That air case is in the way of the rowers, and the builders will have to put that right. But I reckon she won't let us down."

"Who do you reckon will be cox, then?" asked Dick.

"There's to be a meeting about that, February I think. I reckon it'll be Clarke; he's a good man."

The two men continued to wave at the throng as the carriage continued through the streets of Bridlington until the procession reached Trinity Church. There they turned into Trinity Cut, which led to the sands.

Once on the beach, *Seagull* was surrounded by hordes of well-wishers, eager to have a closer look at the new boat.

The crew clambered from the lifeboat and lined up

facing the sea. Photographer Michael Boak arranged his tripod and shouted: "Keep still, everybody!" Kit gazed at the camera until the call "Thank you, gentlemen" allowed him to relax.

Mr Postill, the secretary of the Sailors' and Workingmen's Club, came towards the men and called them together.

"Good news, men. I have a Boxing Day gift for you. Rev. Lloyd-Graeme has awarded you five pounds each for turning out today. Come down to the club tomorrow morning and I'll let you have the money."

"Thanks, Mr Postill," Kit said, "Thank him for us will you? Come on, men, let's have three cheers for Rev. Lloyd-Graeme. Hip! Hip!"

The crew members all bellowed "Hooray!" and clapped each other on the shoulders.

Kit looked back at the *Seagull* and remembered the meeting when the tragedy of 10th February was discussed. Of the forty-two men there, thirty-seven of them claimed the National boat was too high and bulky for working from a flat beach like Bridlington. Kit had cast his vote for a boat design that now stood before him. But the Institution had still refused to take on the boat and she was now in the care of the Sailors' and Workingmen's Club.

Kit remembered gasping when the announcement was made that the cost for *Seagull* and her carriage – and the new boathouse with the ground it was built on – was eight hundred pounds. To Kit it was a fortune, but he was pleased that such a fine boat had been built for the fishermen of Bridlington.

He hoped no-one would be lost at sea when the *Seagull* was on duty.

Chapter 14

15 October 1892

"Come on, Kit, there's hell on down at pier!" Dick Purvis charged into Kit Brown's warehouse, his face red with exertion.

"What's happened then!" Kit Brown put down the net he was repairing and came to the door.

The two men looked out to Bridlington Bay where the waves were still high in the aftermath of an autumn gale.

"The *William Parker*'s still out there and the captain's saying we intend to steal it off him. He's talking to Yonge now. Apparently he's claiming that the lifeboatmen offered to take him back to the boat when it faired up a bit. Now, someone's asking for ten pounds to take him and his crew back to the boat. The captain is playing hell with Lieutenant Yonge and Captain Atkin, accusing us of trying to steal his boat."

"Steal his boat? How the hell can we steal his boat?" Kit looked puzzled.

"Well, if the boat is unmanned the lifeboat could claim it as salvage. And if they did that, the captain would be right. I mean, he claims the men in the lifeboat said he'd be taken back when the weather improved."

"What can we do, then?"

"Dunno, but coxswain says it wasn't him that encouraged the crew to leave the boat." Dick Purvis turned to leave, and added, "But we'd better get down there. You know what those young 'uns on the boat are like. Act first, think afterwards."

Kit took his jacket off the hook on the warehouse door and the two men walked up Spring Pump Slipway to Cliff Street.

When they arrived at the north pier, they could see a crowd of men by the landing steps. There appeared to be two or three men in the middle facing another score or so, all gesticulating and shouting.

Kit and Dick ran down the steps and pushed their way through the crowd.

"OK, lads, let's be through!" Kit shouted. "Morning Captain, morning Lieutenant Yonge." Kit touched his forehead as a sign of respect. "What's to do?"

"Morning Kit," said Captain Atkin. "We've a problem. Captain Wilson, of the *William Parker*, reckons the lifeboat crew offered to return him and his crew to the boat. But now Captain Wilson claims he's been asked to pay ten pounds for the return trip. The Captain says it appears to him that we persuaded him to leave the boat so that local men could claim salvage. That's a serious accusation, Kit." Captain Atkin glared at the men in front of him.

"Come on, Captain, I don't see that could be right. What does the cox say?"

"He says he didn't know the crew encouraged the men to leave the *William Parker*. He was busy controlling the lifeboat. The tide was strong and although the *William Parker* wasn't beached, waves were breaking over her. He reckons it was bad enough for the boat to be abandoned. Now the captain said it wasn't that bad."

Kit turned to the crowd of men. "Do any of you know what happened?"

"Aye, I do." A man pushed his way through the crowd of men to stand in front of Kit Brown.

"If Lieutenant Yonge doesn't know this man, it's Alf Charlton. Right, Alf, speak up."

"Well, I was up front of the lifeboat and I heard nowt about advising the captain to get off the boat. Bob Wallis told me he was happy the captain and the crew left the boat as it was in a dangerous position. He offered to take the captain back and asked for ten pounds for the service. That was when *William Parker*'s captain told us he expected to be returned without anything to pay. He said the crew had told him that would be OK." Alf Charlton stepped back into the crowd.

Another man pushed his way to the front. He said: "I heard as how the Coastguard chief reckoned the boat was not in danger. The weather was improving. The *William Parker* had survived the night and he thought there was no danger. Well, that's what I heard." He turned and disappeared into the crowd.

Alf Charlton turned and spoke again: "Someone told me that the crew seemed surprised when the lifeboat turned up. They weren't ready to leave their boat and had to go below for their bags of clothing. If your boat's in danger you're usually ready to leave it. But they weren't. I don't understand it at all."

Captain Atkin said: "There'll be a committee meeting in a day or so to find out what happened. You men had better get your stories right. We don't want another shadow to fall on the lifeboat service here in Bridlington. Go home men. Lieutenant Yonge and I have work to do."

As Atkin and the Lieutenant turned away, there was a scuffle in the crowd and within a few seconds men had formed a circle round two fighting men.

"What now?" Kit asked Dick. "This lot can't do a thing right."

Kit and Dick pushed to the front of the circle and saw two youths pummelling each other on the ground.

There was no word from either, just grunts of pain and shouts of success. Kit and Dick watched the pair, glancing at each other and then back at the fighting men.

One of the youths swung a round-house blow at the other and the latter fell to the ground, trembled, then lay still.

The victor stood up and brushed his jacket and trousers to remove the dirt of the pier.

"Fred!" Kit Brown shouted. "What the hell are you doing now?"

"He accused us of trying to steal his boat, so I hit him." Fred stood with a defiant stance before his father.

"Oh! So you just hit him, did you? Did you listen to his side of the story? Have you learned anything I've told you, you young hooligan. My God Fred, you'll be the death of me if you don't grow up and act your age."

The fallen fighter had regained his feet but was swaying as he struggled to keep his balance.

"Here lad," Kit Brown said as he held out a hand. "Fred here has something to say."

"What?" questioned Fred.

"Tell the fellow you're sorry, for a start." Kit tugged at Fred's shoulder to bring him closer.

"But I'm not sorry. Not after what he said," Fred put his hands behind his back.

"Fred, shake hands with him and apologise, or I'll make you sorry."

Mumbling to himself, Fred reached out a hand and finally said: "Sorry, mate."

The other man looked Fred in the eye: "Me too. You're a lifeboatman and sailors shouldn't fall out with lifeboatmen."

"Just a minute! Who says *he's* a lifeboatman?" Kit pointed at Fred.

"He did," the man replied, nodding at Fred. "When I criticised what was going on here."

"He told you he was a lifeboatman?" Kit shook his head slowly and turned to Fred.

"You want to be a lifeboatman and I find you fighting on the pier. Oh! Grow up, Fred! Get yourself home, now!" Kit shouted the last word and Fred left, with his head down and feet hardly leaving the ground.

"Right," Kit said. "I suggest we all go home." He turned to address Captain Atkin. "There'll be a meeting to find out about all this, then, Captain?"

"Yes, Brown. In a couple of days. You'd think by now we'd have got these disputes solved once and for all. God knows where the lifeboat service in Bridlington is going. It seems to get worse."

Chapter 15

3 November 1892

"Dick Purvis got me out of bed at quarter to six that morning," started Bob Wallis, at the adjourned committee meeting of the Sailors' and Workingmen's Club. "He told me there was a vessel ashore to the south. From the boathouse I couldn't see whether she was aground or not. She certainly looked in danger and I decided to launch the boat. I sent for Captain Atkin. After we launched and got nearer the boat I saw she was afloat. Some of the lifeboat crew suggested that the captain and crew should be advised to leave her as she was in a dangerous position. There was a strong sea running even though the wind had fallen.

"When we got close to her we went alongside and the captain came on deck. The crew asked him if he was going to leave and if he did so he would be put back. The captain and crew did come onto the lifeboat, but I didn't hear the captain agree it was on the understanding that he would be put back.

"The next day I saw the captain, and he said he wanted to go back. It was still dangerous to launch, as the north wind was blowing strong, and the vessel was in a dangerous situation. I asked him for ten pounds to take him and the crew back."

"And what did the captain say to that, Mr Wallis?" asked Captain Atkin.

"He refused to pay. When I saw him the next day I asked for six pounds as the weather was a little better. But he wouldn't pay that either. Later in the day I asked for five pounds. But he maintained that we'd agreed to take him back when he wanted to. That was the condition on which he left his vessel. I say that the *William Parker* was in danger when I took him off. The waves were still breaking on her and I have learned that one anchor had parted during the night."

"Anything else, Wallis?"

"Yes, sir. I don't think it's right to say that the crew promised to take him back."

"Did you go along with that?"

"Well, no sir, I was too busy controlling the boat. There was a big sea running at the time, remember."

"Thank you, Wallis. Mr Charlton?"

Albert Charlton came forward and offered what he knew about the incident.

After his evidence, the committee huddled to consider their next steps.

Lieutenant Yonge, the committee chairman, then announced: "It is the opinion of this committee that neither crew nor cox of our lifeboats should actively persuade captains or crews to leave their vessels. That decision must be taken by those in danger. We offer help only. Not advice. Having said that, it is ludicrous to think that members of Bridlington's lifeboat service would deliberately set out to persuade a captain and crew to leave a ship in a hazardous position so that they could return and claim it as salvage.

"Let us hope this is the end of another unsavoury incident in the lifeboat service of Bridlington."

Chapter 16

8 February 1893

"You can't refuse." Captain Atkin's red face glowered at the fishermen on the beach. "You're lifeboatmen, you've got to practice."

"We will, but the launch crew have a point," a voice shouted.

"What? You mean you agree that they should get the same money as the boat crew?"

"Why not?" Wilf Tanner strode to stand in front of Captain Atkin. "We've got to man the ropes waist deep in freezing water sometimes and our work is more physical than theirs."

"How can you say that?" the Captain retorted. "It's the crew that have to man the oars, and they're at sea for an hour at a time. The launch crew can go home and change while they're still out there."

The crowd of fishermen surrounded Captain Atkin, the lifeboat crew clambering over the sides of the *Seagull* to add to the clamour.

"We reckon we're worth four bob the same as the crew, and we're not going to launch her until you agree," Wilf Tanner shouted.

"I can't change the rules," Captain Atkin said.

"You're lifeboat secretary. You could if you wanted."

"No I can't. We need to vote on it in committee at the Club," Captain Atkin tried to expain.

"To hell with your committee," shouted Wilf. "I ain't helping to launch this boat unless I get the same as them in the crew." He folded his arms as if to put an end to the discussion.

"How do the rest of you feel?" Captain Atkin looked at the crew of the lifeboat, shuffling their feet, easing their cork jackets on their shoulders, and looking at each other.

Kit Brown walked to the front of the men and said, "I think they've a point, Captain. It's worth you paying up this once. What will happen if we don't practice. We're not going to be much good in a rescue. Then we can discuss it at the next committee meeting."

Several voices joined in backing Kit Brown's view.

Another voice called from the crowd. "I reckon we deserve the same pay. There's times I go home frozen stiff and I've only been in the water a few minutes. And it's bloody hard work too. She might be light on the water, but she's heavy when she's on land. I mean it takes six horses to drag her over the sand and you expect men like me to haul her off the carriage. We're worth four bob any day."

"I've said I can't change the rules. You have to accept what's agreed. It's four bob for the lifeboat crew and two bob for them as launch. And that's that." Captain Atkin tried to push his way through the men.

"I'm not launching this boat," shouted Wilf Tanner, immediately followed by another voice, "Me neither. You can stuff your two bob."

Kit Brown and Dick Purvis moved towards Captain Atkin. Kit shouted: "Let's do this properly, men. Let's practice today and talk about it at the Club."

"No, Kit. It's all right for you. You always get four bob for your work. I've to settle for two. It's not fair." Wilf Tanner seemed to relish being the spokesman for the launch crew.

"If you lot won't accept what I say," Captain Atkin shouted, "then I'm ordering you to take the boat back to the lifeboat house. There will be no practice launch today."

He turned on his heel and lurched over the sands towards the wharf.

Kit Brown turned to the launch crew and threw his cork jacket over the side of the lifeboat. "Anybody can be on the launch crew. Women do it, for heaven's sake. Some of you haven't a clue what goes on out there. You may get wet and cold and work hard, but it's much worse out there."

"Aye," said Dick Purvis. "And afterwards all you have to do is walk home. We still have to row the damn boat back here when the job's over. Then she's to be set up again for next time. Once she's in the shed, you lot have finished. But we haven't."

"He's right. We have to check the jackets, see they're not damaged and repair them if they are. The boat might need a repair, and the oars have to be checked. That'll take us another day."

Wilf Tanner threw his bucket on to the sand and said, "Well, if that's what you think of the launch crew, I'm off. And I won't be here next time you have to go out. You can do it yourselves." He turned his back on the men and followed Captain Atkin's footsteps.

"There's another thing." Dick Purvis's voice made the other men turn towards him. "Remember the six from the *Harbinger*. They died in the lifeboat. You lot in the launch crew don't put your life in danger every time the boat goes out. Once we're out there we could lose our lives. After you've let go the ropes, we're on our own. You can't help us then."

Dick turned to Kit and asked, "So what are we off to do?"

"Better get her back in the shed, lads." He turned to Dick, put a hand on his shoulder, and said, "I don't know, Dick, what the hell's come over these people? Once it gets in *Free Press* folks will be slinging mud at us again."

Chapter 17

19 November 1893

"Dad! Dad! Wake up! There's a ship in distress!"

The shout was accompanied by a thumping on the bedroom door. Kit turned towards the sound: "What's up?" he muttered.

"Dad! There's a ship showing a distress flare. Come on!"

As he realised that it was Fred shouting, he swung his legs out of bed. Mary stirred and he murmured, "It's OK, lass!"

Kit dragged on his serge trousers, and found Fred downstairs pulling his oilskin over his shoulders.

"What's up, Fred?" Kit asked, rubbing his fingers through his hair as he struggled to wake up.

"I've been to the end of pier and there's a ship showing a distress flare. I came straight home to tell you. Are we off to the lifeboat?"

"Depends where that boat is," Kit said.

"She's out towards Flamborough Head, just inside Smithwick I'd guess."

"And where's wind?"

"From south, south-east."

"We'll not bother lifeboat, lad, it'll take over long. You go and wake Dick Purvis and Tom Clark. Tell them to come down to the *Swiftsure*. I'll be getting her ready. Then we'll go." Kit started to pull on his gansey.

"What? Four of us?" Fred stared at Kit as though he couldn't believe his ears.

"Yes, lad. We can do it. Off with you."

Kit pulled long woollen socks over his feet, then pushed them into the long thigh boots he took from their place near the fireplace.

Over the dark blue gansey, tight fitting with its oiled

wool, he drew on a thick serge jacket. He tucked the ends of his neckerchief into his gansey and blew out the candle.

As he pulled the door of the cottage closed behind him, Kit felt the sting of sleet on his face. He could hear the howl of the gale through the ropes and stays of cobles in the harbour and knew the waves would be high.

As he hurried along towards the pier, he dodged a couple of slates as they were hurled to the street by the wind.

No-one else was about as he strode past the *Britannia Inn* on Cliff Street. When he arrived at the steps to the pier, the full force of the gale tugged at him. He took the steps two at a time, and ran across the pier to the landing stage.

In the turgid water of Bridlington harbour, the coble *Swiftsure* pulled at her moorings. The cobles followed a traditional wooden East Coast design, having iron-shod keels so they could be pulled on to sand or shingle. Local craftsmen had built all these cobles, the backbone of the local fishing fleet. Clinker-built, with a jib sheet and a mainsail, the biggest being up to forty feet in length, they filled one corner of Bridlington harbour. *Swiftsure*'s owner, Sid Champlin, allowed Kit to use the vessel whenever he needed, and Kit knew there would be no problem in borrowing the coble for an errand of mercy.

He had been on the boat only a few minutes when he heard running feet approaching within the moans of the easterly gale.

"Ey up, Kit! What's to do?" asked Dick Purvis.

"Someone's in trouble out there. Showing a flare. It'll be a bad 'un tonight, but thought we'd be better off in a coble than call the lifeboat. Don't want to be caught up in another row with Atkin." Kit busied himself with the sail as Dick hoisted the rudder in place.

Two minutes later, three more men ran up. Fred's face was bursting with excitement and he shouted: "I've got Tom Clark, Dad, and we met Jack Usher, and he's come and all." The three men jumped onto the coble and Kit

70

loosed the rope tying her to the jetty and the wind caught the sail.

"Better make her fully reefed, Dick. Shan't need much sail tonight." Kit turned to Jack and asked: "How come you were out?"

"I couldn't sleep. Windows were rattling, so I got up to look outside. I'd just opened door when your lad came belting past. I asked what was up, and he said you were off to rescue somebody.

"He said he were off for Tom so I thought I might as well come and all."

"Extra pair of hands won't come amiss tonight, Kit," Tom said. "Looks as though it might be a rough 'un."

"Aye," said Kit. "Look sharp then, lads. Let's see if we can do what the lifeboat's supposed to do."

Chapter 18

20 November 1893

The cottage door of 3 Spring Pump Slipway eased open and Kit and Fred Brown tiptoed into the small front room. A candle was spluttering in its holder in the middle of the scrubbed table top throwing deep shadows round the room.

In the grate a few coals glowed, and a wisp of steam spiralled towards the ceiling from the spout of a large black kettle. Mary Brown was slumped in a rocking chair by the fireside. She opened her eyes at the slight noises and looked round.

"Oh! Kit! You're safe! And you, too, Fred! Thank God!" She held out her arms to her husband and clung to him.

"It's OK, lass, we're fine," Kit hugged Mary and then sat at the table. Kit sat in the rocking chair, unlacing his boots.

"I heard you go. I knew something must be wrong, so I got up and put kettle on. I'll make a cup of tea. Do you want anything to eat?" Mary busied herself with making tea, and Kit threw his boots under the table.

Fred Brown, his face reflecting the excitement he felt, started to speak. "It was awesome, Mam! That storm, well, them waves were like mountains. But we . . ." and Fred pointed to his father and then stuck his thumb into his chest, "rescued the crew." He leaned back on his chair, with a wide smile on his face.

"Aye, Fred, we did. But *you've* a lot to learn!" Kit thrust his finger at Fred.

"I was all right, Dad. I knew what I was doing." Fred's smile disappeared.

"Oh, you did, did you? What about all those times I've told you about safety? About how you have to think? You didn't think! You just thought you'd be a dashing hero but ended up looking stupid. Did you see the way Dick and Tom looked at you as you went onto the *Victoria*? No, you were too busy being clever. They knew you weren't doing things right, but they said nowt because I was there."

"But Dad . . ." Fred started.

"Now you listen here, Fred. It's time you learned that being a hero isn't something you do. It's something you are. And things happen to make heroes. *You* don't make it happen." Kit stood up at the table and banged his fist as he spoke.

"Kit . . ." Mary turned from the fireplace and approached Kit, her hand stretched towards him, to calm him.

"Make the tea, lass. This is between him and me. Not you." Kit glowered at her and Mary turned back to making the tea.

"So you knew what you were doing, eh?" Kit stared down at his son. "You knew the boats were secure? You knew someone was at the tiller? You knew that the sail was loose? And you'd checked the sea to make sure there were no rogue waves coming behind you?" Kit's voice held a sneer.

"I didn't need to. I knew you'd be doing all that," Fred said. "So I could leave *Swiftsure* and go onto the *Victoria*."

"But did you look to see if I was still at the tiller? No! You just thought you'd do it, and leapt to the other boat. What if a wave had knocked me off my feet just as you jumped, and the *Swiftsure* had moved away from *Victoria*? You'd never have made it. Like as not you'd have drowned. So much for helping fellow seamen. Useless, you were. I know you brought a couple of men out, but we'd have got them anyway.

"Nay, lad, you've a lot to learn." Kit sat down again and put his head on the table. He felt exhausted now he was home. He turned to Mary and said: "How's that tea coming on, lass? I'll have that, then I'm off to bed. I'm worn out."

Mary passed him a mug full of dark brown tea, then another mug to Fred.

"But, Mam. I was all right, really. It worked out right in the end, didn't it?" He started to smile again. "I bet there's medals for us," and he indicated where he would pin his.

"Medals? Medals?" Kit sat straight up, banged on the table and tea spilled over the side of his mug. "Is that all you care about? A medal? Look lad, it's not about winning medals, it's about saving lives. How would you like to be in a sinking boat like the *Victoria* and think that all the man who rescues you is concerned about is getting a medal? I'd be hoping he was thinking of me, a fellow sailor, with his life in danger, and making sure he got me to safety. A medal should be the last thing on your mind, Fred. That makes a mockery of the whole life-saving service."

"But, Kit, Fred was only doing what he thought was right." Mary Brown came to the table and sat down, a mug of tea cupped in her hands.

"Aye, Mary. But Fred has to learn that he should be doing what he *knows* is right, not what he *thinks* is right. There's a heck of a difference between the two. If he'd *known* what he was doing, he'd have waited till I told him to go on board the *Victoria*. But he went when he *thought* it was the time to go. And though he got away with it, he were wrong." Kit looked into each face as he spoke, Mary listening intently, Fred with an air of assurance in his ability.

"But, Dad, no-one but those on board know what happened. You're not going to tell anyone about it are you? I mean . . ." Fred's voiced tailed off.

"You mean if everyone knows what really happened, they'd tell you you were wrong. Well, no, I shan't say anything about that. It wouldn't do any good, and it wouldn't change anything. The men were saved, and that's what we went out for."

Kit drank the rest of his tea, and started to stand up, but then sat down again.

"Fred. There could be bother about this, you know," Kit's voice was now calm. "You realise that because we rescued the men, the lifeboat crew weren't called. Some of your mates may think we denied them their money for a launch. So don't go bragging about how brave you were. Other men will think that all you did was take brass out of their pockets.

"Some folk will praise us for what we did. Others will still say the lifeboat should have been called. They may be right. After all, that's what it's there for. Maybe I didn't have any right to do what I did. All I know is those sailors would have drowned if we'd had to wait for the lifeboat. Others won't see it that way, though." Kit gazed into space, as he visualised the response of his fellow fishermen when they learned about the rescue.

"Oh, Kit. There won't be any trouble will there?" Mary reached for Kit's hands and gripped them.

"Can't say, lass, that I can't. But I'm off upstairs to bed. You'd better get to bed, too, Fred. There's still work to be done at first light." Kit pecked Mary on her cheek, found another candle, lit it from the one on the table, and left the room.

Fred crossed the room to the rocking chair, stretched his legs and wriggled his toes in the warmth of the fire. He put his hands behind his head, and let a smile of self-satisfaction spread over his face.

"I might get a medal," he whispered, so his mother didn't hear him. "A medal for a hero."

Chapter 19

20 November 1893

Kit Brown turned the corner of King Street and collided with the last man he wanted to see that morning.

"Morning, Brown."

"Captain."

Captain Atkin barred Kit's path and stood like a statue. "I hear you did a good job last night."

"Aye, thanks, Captain. I think we did." Kit Brown made to pass the other man, but Atkin moved to bar his path again.

"I'd like to know why you didn't think to call the lifeboat." Captain Atkin stood his ground and glared into Kit Brown's face.

"I did think about it, Captain. But not for long. I thought we could do the job with a coble and we did." Once again Kit made to evade the Captain. "Excuse me, Captain, this is not the place."

"It might not, Brown, but it's the right time. Why didn't you call me for the lifeboat?"

"Look, I saw the distress flare so I took the coble. I had no second thoughts."

"But a coble's not a lifeboat, man. You should have called the lifeboat!"

"What? By the time you'd walked to seawall, made your mind up, called the crew and the horses, got the boat to the beach and pulled off, that schooner would have been a gonner." Kit's voice gradually became more heated.

"But that's the lifeboat's job, man!" Captain Atkin spluttered.

"So it is. But I knew yon schooner was in trouble and we hadn't time to call you. I went straight down to the harbour and commandeered the *Swiftsure*. I knew Sid

Champlin wouldn't mind. Fred went off for Dick and Tom and came back with Jack as well."

"Yes, yes, yes. But you undermined my position as Lifeboat Secretary, you know. And I can't have that." Captain Atkin drew himself up to his full height and straightened his tie.

"I can see why you think that way, Captain. But there wasn't enough time. So I took the coble. And we were successful, don't forget that."

The two men started walking down King Street, and they crossed Cross Street, before ambling down Spring Pump Slipway towards Kit's cottage.

"The committee will have words about this you know, Brown. I don't think they'll take kindly to you deciding to take the coble."

"Look, Captain. I can't help what they think. I took the coble. I knew it was right. And I was right. We rescued those men from the *Victoria* just before it sank. The lifeboat would have been too late. And that would have been another controversy for Bridlington men."

Chapter 20

2 December 1893

A clatter at the door knocker broke into Mary Brown's doze. She woke to hear the kettle still hissing on the hob and the deep tick of Kit's grandfather clock in the corner. She rubbed her eyes and realised what had disturbed her.

"Hang on a minute," she called and struggled to her feet, the baby heavy beneath her apron. She pulled her shawl round her shoulders and waddled to the door. On opening it she found no-one standing there, only one or two women passing down Spring Pump Slipway. She glanced up the hill to make sure then down to the harbour. Across the hill a line of people waited to fill their buckets with spring water.

Mary shook her head in bewilderment and went back indoors. As she shut the door she noticed a tightly folded piece of paper under the door curtain. She stooped to pick it and took it back to her chair. Unfolding the paper she looked at the words. In large badly formed capitals the writing said: "Your husband stole my Wilfred's money. Some of us think what he did was wrong."

Mary turned the paper over but there was nothing else to see. She read it again but didn't understand what it meant. As far as she knew, Kit had never done a dishonest deed in his life.

Mary pondered. "Wilfred," she said, "Wilfred who?"

Her hands dropped into her lap and she ran through all the names she knew at the Quay. There were many because she had lived at number three since she was a girl of eighteen and married Kit. The only Wilfred she could think of was Wilf Tanner. It couldn't be him, she thought. He had married her friend Aggie. Kit and Wilf often had a pint together in the *Coble & Anchor* and she and Aggie had children of the same age at the Board School.

She was thinking about Wilf and Aggie when Kit came into the room. He hung his jacket on the back of the door and came over to Mary. "Hello, lass," he said, and bent down to kiss her cheek.

"Have a look at this, Kit," Mary said, offering him the piece of paper.

"What is it?" he asked.

"I don't know what to make of it," Mary replied. "It came through the door a few minutes ago."

"It says Wilfred. Wilfred who?" asked Kit.

"I wondered if it was Wilf Tanner," suggested Mary, putting crockery on the table.

"Wilf Tanner? Why Wilf Tanner?" Kit sat at the table and started to pull off his sea boots.

"He's the only Wilf I know," said Mary.

The fire crackled and the kettle hissed again.

"Mug of tea, Kit?"

"Aye, love, thanks. Wilf Tanner. Mind you . . ." he started.

"Go on," Mary said, reaching to the dresser for mugs.

"He were a bit off at pub today. I thought something must have upset him. He wouldn't let me buy him a pint and he's never refused before."

Mary poured dark brown tea into Kit's mug and said, "It could be him then. But what's the money about?"

"Don't know, lass," Kit replied, gulping his tea. "He were always a bit odd if anything went wrong. I think he's still narked because I didn't call him when we went for the *Victoria*."

Mary sat up straight and said, "I bet that's it. He's on lifeboat, isn't he?"

"Aye."

"So he didn't go with you and he didn't go on lifeboat either because it didn't go out."

"So?"

"Well, Aggie will reckon you've taken his four bob launch fee. He'd've got that if you'd called lifeboat, wouldn't he?"

79

"Aye, lass, he would. By heck, thou's a bright one." Kit leaned towards her and pecked her lips.

"Do you reckon it was Aggie that wrote the note?" Mary asked.

Kit swallowed the last of his tea and nodded. "Aye, reckon it was. What shall you do about it?"

"Me?" There was surprise in Mary's voice. "Me? I'm doing nowt. She might be a friend but I'm not wanting to be on wrong side of her. She can make trouble, she can."

Kit looked at Mary. "But note's for you. It's up to you to do something."

"Right," said Mary. "I'll do something then," and she leaned towards the fireplace. She held the paper over the flames and dropped it. The paper flared and the ashes floated up the chimney.

"There," she said. "That's the end of that!"

Mary winced, then slumped into her chair, resting her hands on the bulge of the baby.

Kit glanced at his wife, wishing the lifeboat's problems could be burned to fly up the chimney.

Chapter 21

10 December 1893

In the shadow of the south pier, the fisherwomen of Bridlington huddled together in the early December chill. In their black shawls, skirts and lace-up boots they moved slowly on the slippery rocks.

At their feet were baskets into which they threw limpets they hacked from the seawall. Most of them wielded sharp knives to cut the shellfish from its root. The work was wearying and two women at the pier end stopped working and turned towards each other.

"Sorry to hear you lost one of the twins, Mary." Betsy Purvis put her knife into her apron pocket.

"Aye. Thanks, lass. She would have been a bonny wee thing. Dr Nelson has no idea why she died. He just shrugged his shoulders." Mary brushed away a tear. "But at least I've got our Kitty."

Betsy put an arm round her friend's shoulder and let Mary weep.

"I'd love to have seen her grow up. She'd have been a real treasure. But she's gone and there's nowt we can do about that now. It would have been nice to have two lasses grow up together." Mary wiped her face with the edge of her apron. The two women fell silent for a few moments.

"Have you seen owt of Aggie Tanner?" Betsy asked.

"No," replied Mary. "I thought she'd have come round when I lost the bairn but I've not seen her. Is there owt up with her?"

Betsy Purvis looked at the other women as they plucked the bait from the wall. "I heard as how she played hell with her Wilf about not going out on the lifeboat the other night."

"What? When Kit went out?" Mary looked surprised.

"Aye. Apparently Wilf was ranting a bit after he and some of the other fishermen had been in the *Coble & Anchor*. Some of them reckon Kit stole their money."

Mary murmured: "So it was her that wrote the letter."

Betsy said: "Letter? What letter?"

"It was a letter saying that Kit had stolen her Wilf's money, and that what Kit did was wrong."

"Stole his money? But that's . . ."

"Aye, Mary. That's crazy. But that's what were in the letter. And now you say Aggie said it to Wilf. I bet Wilf started saying as how Kit should have called the lifeboat, never mind how long it took. Then he would have got his four shillings for launching."

"But," said Mary, "The men in the *Victoria* would have drowned."

"Aye, we know that. That's what Dick said, too. I don't know, some folk have no idea." Betsy Purvis shook her head in dismay.

Both women took their knives and started cutting the limpets from the wall. They had worked without speaking for several minutes when a group of other women approached them.

The leader of the group, a bulky woman in the black of fisherwives, shouted: "I want a word with you, Mary Brown."

Mary and Betsy looked at each and then at the woman.

"Aye, you, Mary Brown. It weren't fair of your Kit to take yon coble out on that rescue. He did my Wilf out of his four bob. It's all right for your man now, Mary Brown. He's had plenty of brass given him. But my Wilf is as brave as him and deserves his bit. You want to tell your man that we don't agree with what's happened."

Aggie Tanner's voice lost some of its initial aggression but she still shook a fist at Mary and Betsy to emphasise what she had to say.

"And shall I tell him about the letter saying he stole your . . ." started Mary.

"Letter? Letter? I don't know anything about a letter.

82

Anyway why would anyone say it were my Wilf complaining?"

Mary knew then that Aggie had sent the letter, but decided not inflame her further. "Kit went to rescue those in trouble. He did what he reckoned was right."

"Oh, aye, you'll be making smart excuses for him no doubt. But you're the one with new boots on your kids' feet. Mine are still wearing their old ones. And, like as not, they'll be wearing them a while yet. Don't think we don't know about the collection from the *Chronicle.*" Aggie's anger started to boil again.

"Look, Aggie, we've been friends . . ."

"Have been," sneered Aggie. "That's right enough. Have been." And she started to turn away from Mary.

"But Aggie it's nowt to do with us. And you know it. Our men do what they have to do and they'll never think of what it means to us." Mary tried to placate Aggie.

"Oh, so you admit he may have been wrong?" Aggie leaned forward, anger reddening her face.

"Look, Aggie, I don't know whether what he did was right. But he's my man and I support him. I know he risked his life for those men in the *Victoria*. And Betsy's Dick did too. And the others. Don't forget our Fred was with them. I could have lost my husband and my eldest son." Mary's shoulders drooped as she realised what her loss could have been.

"Come on, Aggie. You'd have been on your Wilf's side if he'd gone out. And you'd be glad of the extra brass. But compared with losing your man that brass is not enough."

While the women were shouting at each other, others had joined them and the group had swelled.

"My Francis missed his four bob too, don't forget, Mary." A young woman stepped forward, her skirt bulging with her unborn baby. "We need some stuff for the bairn when it comes. Now we can't have it."

"Amy, I'm sorry for your hard times but I can't make amends, can I? I've no spare brass you know. Kit wants his money for a new coble and he needs that to get us a living from the sea. But I'll tell you what. Come to the cottage and I'll let you have a shawl that was for the bairn I lost."

"You can't get out of it, Mary Brown," Aggie Tanner shouted.

Amy butted in and said: "But I'll have that shawl. Thanks Mary. Maybe we'd better start thinking about each other instead of falling out like this. We're all in the same boat really."

Another woman stepped out and said: "This arguing is not getting the bait in. My Jack will play hell with me if I don't get two baskets by sunset. I'm off back to work."

She split away from the group and walked slowly along the base of the pier. In ones and twos others followed until there was only a handful left.

"Come on, Mary," said Betsy, "We won't change their minds. And they don't want to listen to our side."

Aggie turned to move away. "Don't think you've heard the last of this, Mary Brown. My Wilf says there's a meeting of the lifeboat committee tomorrow and Kit'll be put in his place. Wilf is as much of a hero as he is." Aggie was still shaking her fist as she left Mary and Betsy.

Within a few minutes, all the women were at work, hacking and cutting limpets from the cold stone of Bridlington's harbour walls.

Chapter 22

11 December 1893

"This meeting of the Life Boat Sub-Committee of the Sailors' and Workingmen's Club is now in session, Captain Thomas Atkin in the chair."

The crowded room became silent as the captain banged his gavel on the table.

Captain Atkin gained his feet with care, favouring his left leg. He looked around the room before speaking. "I have called this special meeting so that full discussion may be made of the incident of 28 November last. Late that night, a member of the lifeboat crew took it upon himself to borrow a vessel without permission and launch into dreadful seas in an effort to save the crew of a sinking ship."

He paused and looked straight at Kit Brown, seated at the end of the front row before him.

"The rescue of five men from certain death is not the issue here today. The issue is whether Brown acted in a manner becoming the lifeboat service and the seamen of this town. We shall hear from others involved in this incident. Gentlemen, it is likely to be an acrimonious meeting, as there are totally opposing views to be heard. I urge you to control your feelings, have respect for your fellow man and listen to all that is said.

"For the sake of the record I shall name the committee here today. They are: Messrs. R. Hopper, J. W. Postill, M. Walkington, D. Walkington, J. Allerston, J. Knaggs, E. Wardill, J. W. Harrison, J. H. Sawden and L. Pipes."

Captain Atkin eased himself into the arms of the wooden chair at the centre of the table and gestured to the secretary. John Postill stood up, straightened himself, unfastened the top button of his waistcoat and then mopped his forehead.

"Gentlemen. The facts are these: On the night of 28 November last, Fred Brown, Kit Brown's son, took the news home that a vessel was showing a distress flare. Kit Brown, Fred and three others, took the coble *Swiftsure* and sailed into the night to rescue the crew of the schooner *Victoria*. She sank immediately upon the crew being rescued. The crew was brought to harbour in safety and lodged at the *Waterloo Café* for the rest of the night.

"These facts are supported by the captain of the *Victoria*, Captain John William Constable. He will have his opportunity to speak later.

"Kit Brown has already given details of the rescue to this sub-committee and these details are supported by his son Fred, Dick Purvis, Tom Clark, and Jack Usher.

"There has been much discussion about whether the *Swiftsure* should have been taken by Brown without the permission of the owner, Sid Champlin. Brown assures us that he has full permission to use that particular vessel and reasoned that Sid Champlin would have no objection to the vessel's use on such an errand of mercy.

"I'd like to ask Kit Brown if there is anything further to add," John Postill sat down and breathed a sigh of relief.

All eyes turned as Kit Brown left his chair and walked to the front of the table. He ran his hand over his greying hair and turned to the men before him.

"Now you all know me. I've been a fisherman in the port of Bridlington for many a long year. There's not a lot I don't know about the sea hereabouts. On that night my lad Fred called me from my bed with the news that a boat was in distress. By the time we made the north pier, it was obvious that the vessel would not stay afloat for long. She appeared to be at the north-east end of the Smithwick. There was a fierce gale blowing from the south and to my mind that vessel would be blown onto Sewerby rocks in less than an hour."

Kit Brown drew a handkerchief from his trouser pocket and wiped his face, moustache and beard. He continued: "I know how long it takes to launch the lifeboat. There are times when it has taken but twenty minutes to get the boat in the water, but there also have been times when nigh on an hour has passed before the keel touches the tide."

A voice roared from the back of the hall: "Rubbish, Brown, and you know it."

Captain Atkin thrashed the table top with the gavel. "Be quiet. Let Brown speak." He gestured to Kit Brown with the gavel. "Go on, Brown."

"As I said, on some occasions it takes the lifeboat a long time to be launched. I reckoned the rescue could be done by a coble. Sailing in cobles is something we do each and every day. So I took the *Swiftsure*. To ask permission would have wasted even more time. Then we did what we could. I have said this once and will say it again: 'Bridlington men never turn their backs on mariners in trouble.' The men were rescued. We went home to bed."

A cry from the other side of the room swelled above the noise: "Well done, Brown. Well done."

Mr Postill then called on Dick Purvis and the other three men of the crew of the *Swiftsure*. All gave support to Kit Brown's words. When young Fred Brown had finished speaking, there were wide grins of approval showing round the room. But there were also some angry faces and bunched fists.

"Can I say something, Captain Atkin?" A man rose from his seat in the centre of the room.

Captain Atkin waved a hand in permission.

"I'd like to know," said the man, looking round the room as he spoke, "why Kit Brown thought he should not call the lifeboat? He's been a member of the crew on many occasions and has earned his four shilling launch fee every time. Did he not think of his fellow mariners? Was his mind on the rewards that may result from his one-man adventure?"

The speaker sat down amid a buzz of conversation.

Captain Atkin stood up. "I'm sure Brown was thinking only of those men in a stricken ship. But he can say his piece if he so wishes. Kit."

Kit took to his feet again and faced the crowded room. "All I knew was that the lifeboat couldn't have saved the crew of the *Victoria* because she would have sunk before it arrived and the crew would have perished. If anyone thinks I had any other reason than saving lives at sea, he can say it to my face – outside after this meeting. The thought of reward never entered my head. Only that if I can save lives in peril then I will do so. Lives were in peril and I was able to save them. What happened after that I had no control over." Kit Brown sat down again.

The man in the centre stood up. "I suppose Mr Brown is referring to the rewards made to him for his bravery. It must be very nice to be the recipient of purses of gold and silver from the people of Manchester and London. I wish I'd had the chance to earn four bob that night. But no, that was snatched from me by Brown." His last words were shouted at Kit Brown, who flinched at the onslaught.

"Mr Chairman . . ." Kit began.

"A moment, Kit. Let him continue." He turned to the accuser. "Have you anything else to say?"

"Yes, I have. Many of us know why Brown went out that night. After his cowardice during the Great Gale when he was 'resting' when the *Harbinger* turned over and six of the crew drowned, he has tried to ingratiate himself back into the lifeboat community. He was one of the crew who refused to practice that year. And here he is now going out alone on a rescue, denying the lifeboatmen of their rightful reward."

Several voices muttered: "Aye."

"I fail to see that a man accused of cowardice would sail out into a raging sea in a coble," said Captain Atkin. "To me, that shows bravery beyond measure. You, sir, are entitled to your opinion. But opinion only is what it is. The facts remain. Brown indeed acted heroically and, I believe, deserves our wholehearted support."

A tall, thin man at the table gestured at Captain Atkin to speak. Atkin nodded and the man stood up. "You fishermen may not know this yet but I reckon I'm not speaking out of turn when I tell you that the funds of this Institute have had the sum of twenty guineas added. With that extra money we will, in future, be able to be more generous to members who suffer misfortune. I will tell you who donated it, although he was quite certain that no-one would be interested in his generosity. The benefactor was Kit Brown. He offered the money from that given him by the townspeople of Manchester."

Kit Brown sprang to his feet and pointed a forefinger at Captain Atkin. "You told me nowt would be said . . ."

Captain Atkin glared at Kit Brown, who sat down. "Yes, Brown, I agreed that nothing would be said. But in your defence against these accusations, I think it better that it does not remain a secret. And the treasurer had no such agreement with you."

Captain Atkin addressed the whole room. "Gentlemen. I think it is incumbent upon us to record Kit Brown's endeavours in the records. I propose that 'The Life Boat Sub-Committee of the Sailors' and Workingmen's Club offer their congratulations on the heroism shown on the night of 19 November last by our fellow member Mr Christopher Brown.' Do I have a seconder? Mr Hopper. Thank you. Can I have a show of hands that the motion be carried?"

The men at the table looked at the raised hands, and nodded to each other.

"The motion is carried." Captain Atkin banged his gavel, and leaned back in his chair. He puffed his cheeks as he blew out the tension he'd felt the whole meeting. He closed his eyes for a moment's respite.

When he opened them again, Kit Brown stood in front of him.

"Well, Brown, it's in the minutes now. You have the total support of us all."

"Happen so, Captain. But you were quick to move on and not discuss why the crew went on strike. Didn't want to dwell on that again, did we, Captain?"

Chapter 23

22 December 1893

"I don't think I'll ever do anything like that again!" As she smiled at Fred Brown, Millicent Lloyd-Graeme blushed. "Well, I *have* just kissed the youngest hero I'll ever meet. Even though I'm engaged to be married."

The crowd erupted with a cheer and Millicent sat down. Fred Brown, touching his cheek where Millicent had kissed him, turned to the people in the hall and said: "I'd do it all again for another kiss like that!"

Kit Brown watched as his son bathed in the glow of being a hero. Kit thought back a few minutes to when the first announcements were being made.

Captain Atkin, the lifeboat secretary, stood on the small stage of the Londesborough Hall. "Ladies and gentlemen. It gives me great pleasure this evening to honour five Bridlington men. These brave men, carrying on the great tradition of this town, risked their very lives in saving others from the depths of the sea. With little concern for their own safety, they took a coble and sailed into the teeth of a terrible storm. In pitch blackness, they took that coble through tumultuous waves at the harbour mouth, and approached the stricken *Victoria*. She had sailed from Aberdeen with a cargo of cement. The storm had forced her onto the shelving sands of Bridlington Bay. Her crew had given up all hope of rescue and a watery death loomed before them.

"But Kit Brown, a man who knows well the terrors of the sea, his son Fred, and three fisherman friends, Dick Purvis, Tom Clark and Jack Usher, rescued the whole crew and brought them back to harbour and safety."

As Captain Atkin looked across the stage at the five men waiting at the side, shuffling their feet and passing the rim of their caps through their fingers in embarrassment, applause broke out in the hall.

Captain Atkin held up his hand, and the room became silent again. "Not only did they carry out this amazing rescue, but they told no-one. They went out in the middle of the night, rescued the crew, put them into the *Waterloo Café* for a meal and bed, then," Captain Atkin paused, "and then, just went home. No-one knew they had been out."

Another burst of applause came from the audience, punctuated with whistles and the stamping of feet.

Captain Atkin held out a hand and the eyes of the crowd looked on the five heroes.

Captain Atkin said: "Ladies and gentlemen. The skipper of the coble *Swiftsure* on that terrible night was Christopher Brown, better known to you all as Kit Brown." Captain Atkin stepped back and Kit Brown, his step unsure in his embarrassment, walked to the front of the stage.

Applause filled the building for a full minute, before Captain Atkin once again brought the crowd to silence.

Kit said: "Ladies and gentlemen. You have honoured us this evening. We are but humble men and the sea provides our living. She also claims our friends, but she shall not have them." Kit drew in a deep breath as the crowd applauded. He continued: "We did what we must.

"The Captain called at my cottage the following morning when he learned of the rescue and asked: 'Have you seen the state of the sea?' I had not, and we walked to the pier and looked out into Bridlington Bay. The storm was still in a fury, and huge rollers were sweeping ashore. The bare bones of the *Victoria* were still being swept by terrible waves. I remember turning to the Captain and saying: 'If I had known it was that bad, I might not have gone out. Surely the hand of God was on the tiller last night.'

"But we did rescue those men, and I am sure their wives and families are grateful that we did."

Captain Atkin strode forward and he and Kit shook hands.

"It now gives me great pleasure," said Captain Atkin, "to introduce the Reverend Lloyd-Graeme to award Mr Brown with the sum of ten guineas."

A man in clerical clothing appeared from the wings and ambled to the centre of the stage. In one hand he held a small purse. He held it out to Kit Brown. "Mr Brown, Kit. The people of Bridlington and Bridlington Quay present you with this purse of silver for bravery in the face of great danger while saving lives. It gives me extreme pleasure to shake the hand of a very brave man." As he was speaking, Reverend Lloyd-Graeme shook hands with Kit Brown.

Kit made a nervous bow to Reverend Lloyd-Graeme and mumbled "Thank you, Reverend," before moving back to the side of the stage.

Captain Atkin came centre stage and said: "Reverend Lloyd-Graeme will now make a similar presentation to Dick Purvis, Tom Clark and Jack Usher."

One by one the three men marched to the centre of the stage, shook hands with Reverend Lloyd-Graeme and the Captain, received their purse of silver, then turned to walk back to join Kit.

"Ladies and gentlemen. Our final presentation is to a very young man, perhaps the youngest ever to receive an award like this. And we are honoured to have Miss Millicent Lloyd-Graeme to make the presentation to Fred Brown." As he finished speaking, Captain Atkin's voice rose until he nearly shouted Fred's name.

Fred strode forward, held out his right hand to Captain Atkin, shook the Captain's hand with vigour, and then he turned to Reverend Lloyd-Graeme, clasping his hand in both of his.

Millicent Lloyd-Graeme walked onto the stage, took the purse her father handed her, and stood in front of Fred Brown. She gazed into Fred's face and she smiled at the glimmer of a grin.

"It gives me great pleasure to present this purse of silver to Mr Fred Brown." Millicent put the money in Fred's hand. She glanced at her father, then, putting her hands onto Fred's shoulders, and reaching up on tiptoe, put her lips to Fred's cheek.

As he watched Millicent kiss his son, Kit Brown was remembering how different things could have been.

Chapter 24

9 January 1894

Kit gulped his mug of tea at his usual brief breakfast. He'd already eaten thick slices of bread with meat.

Just as he was reaching for his jacket, there was a knock at the cottage door, and Mary returned with a large envelope, which she handed to her husband. Kit sat down at the table to open it. Mary watched his face as he read the letter, seeing his eyes open in surprise. He looked up at her as she poured more tea into his mug.

"Mary, I have to take my crew to London. It says here I've to catch the nine o'clock train on Tuesday. We'll be met by officials and the Mayor at Kings Cross. Then we've to go to a hall. And," Kit paused as he read the passage again, "and we're to receive two medals."

Kit shouted up the stairs to his son. "Fred! Get yourself out of bed. Go get Dick, Tom and Jack and bring them here straight away."

Fred clattered down the stairs and ran off up the street towards Queens Square. Within five minutes all four had arrived at Kit's cottage.

"What's up, Kit?" Dick Purvis asked through his breathlessness, as he came through the door.

"Aye, what's to do?" Jack Usher wanted to know.

"Sit down, sit down, and I'll tell thee," Kit Brown pushed a chair towards Dick.

"I've got a letter here that says we've to go to London."

"London?" All three men gasped at the same time.

"Aye, London. We're to get medals. Silver medals, it says. And we're to have lunch with the Mayor."

"Does it say anything else?" asked Tom Clark.

"Oh, aye," said Kit. "One medal's from the Board of Trade and the other from the Royal National Lifeboat Institution."

"Bloody hell," said Jack Usher. "We'd better go then."

"Have I to go as well, Dad?" Fred asked.

"Of course, lad, you were part of the crew, weren't you?"

"Well, yes, Dad, but I thought you said . . ." started Fred.

"Never mind what I said." Kit waved a finger at Fred, who was suddenly silent.

"But Kit," said Tom Clark, "I've never been on a train. Will we be all right? I mean, they go so fast."

Dick Purvis smiled: "It'll be all right, Tom. You know there's hundreds of folk come to Brid by train for their holidays. From all over Yorkshire, Wakefield, Sheffield, Leeds, Hull. There's nowt wrong with going by train. You'll be right."

"Oh," said Tom. "It's only 'cos I've heard . . ."

"Don't worry about anything, Tom. We'll all be there, won't we? We'll look after each other. Like we did on the boat," Fred Brown said. He gazed through the window into the distance, murmuring: "A medal. I knew I'd get a medal."

Chapter 25

3 March 1894

"I don't know why you're still on about it, Dad." Fred Brown grabbed the side of the *Elizabeth* as the sea lifted the boat on a wave. "I can't see what the problem is. We need a lifeboat at Bridlington but does it matter which kind?"

"I think it does, Fred. It's all right the Institution dictating to us that we have a self-righter, but there's more to it than that." Kit Brown threw the line out into the heaving seas. "We need a boat that will cope with the conditions here. You know how shallow the Bay is. There's a lot of surf and that's what makes things difficult when we launch." The line uncoiled as Kit watched it disappear into the depths.

The boat was pitching and tossing in rollers which would eventually sweep onto the broad clean sands of Bridlington. Fred gazed over the water at the horizon. The coble shifted uneasily on the sea as the swell lifted and dropped. Every so often the coble tilted as well as lifted. Fred found to his dismay that he was becoming uncomfortable. He looked at his father holding the tiller, his back rigid and his gaze concentrating on the clouds and waves to the north.

Although the morning was cool, Fred suddenly felt clammy and he wiped his forehead with the sleeve of his gansey. He shifted his feet and knew he had to sit down. He moved to the prow of the boat and sat on the board which spanned the boat's width. He felt the sweat on his forehead again, chill in the breeze. He gulped as a rancid taste hit the back of his throat. He swallowed hard and glanced again at his father.

Without warning, his stomach convulsed and the contents flew to spread in the bottom of the boat.

Fred had time to snatch a breath, then he was sick again.

When his body was calm, he looked at his father. Fred knew he wouldn't say anything just then, but he knew what he had to do.

He picked up a bucket, tied a rope to the handle and lowered it into the sea. He swilled the mess away until the boat was clear.

"Better?" Kit Brown asked.

"Aye, Dad."

"I suppose that's last night's boozing? You were late in, and you knew we were off out this morning. Good grief, Fred, when are you going to learn?

"We'd better get them lines in. I reckon there'll be a storm afore long."

They continued to work and the warmth of the early spring sun at noon brought beads of sweat to their foreheads. Fred wiped away the sweat with the back of his hand and turned to his father. He was about to speak when the boat was hit by a larger than normal wave and the suddenness took Fred by surprise. He reached for the gunwhales of the boat, missed, and the momentum of the boat lifting and the weight of his body falling upset his balance. He fell head first over the side into the water.

Kit leapt to where Fred had disappeared. He looked into the sea and the soles of Fred's boots were just above the surface of the water.

Kit grabbed the boots and heaved. Another wave passed under the boat, lifting Fred as the boat dropped. Kit heaved again and brought a spluttering Fred over the side of the coble. He fell into the bottom of the boat, shaking his head and coughing. Kit leaned down to Fred and Fred looked up and screamed: "What the bloody hell did you do that for?"

"What?"

"Tip the boat so I fell overboard. That weren't funny. I bet you did it because I was sick." Fred sat up on the planks in the bowels of the boat and shook his head again. Water sprayed from his hair.

"I didn't tip the boat, Fred," Kit said. "I've just saved your life, you damned fool. If you'd been paying attention instead of day-dreaming you wouldn't have fallen over. I saw the wave coming, but I never thought thou'd go overboard."

"But you should have warned me," Fred shouted.

"Son, you're safe. Leave it," Kit held out his hand to help Fred to his feet.

Fred ignored the hand and stood up, unbalanced as another wave hit the boat.

"No, Dad. You made me look stupid," Fred shouted at his father.

"But who's seen you? We're about as far from other people as we can get. There's only me. What are you worried about, Fred? That I'll go telling everyone? Why would I do that?" Kit looked back at his lines in the sea.

"Because you're always putting me down. I can never do anything right." Fred tipped up his boots and water cascaded to the bottom of the boat.

"It's not that you can never do anything right, Fred. It's that you never bloody learn. All the lessons you've had when things haven't gone right. You haven't changed your attitude or anything. You're still too clever by half." Kit turned towards him. "One day, my lad, your recklessness will be the death of someone. Now come on, we've fish to catch."

The clouds gathering over Bridlington Bay could not match the cloud that fell over father and son as they toiled to take fish from an unwilling sea.

Chapter 26

8 April 1894

The chill of the night air prompted Customs Officer Hythe to push himself further into the doorway of a warehouse at the bottom of Spring Pump Slipway. Hythe was on a mission. He was convinced that some local fishermen were not above smuggling when fishing wasn't good. He'd noticed that not many of the cobles had been to sea for a day or so, a late spring gale keeping them in harbour.

Officer Hythe reflected on what he'd heard earlier that day in the *Coble & Anchor*. While others thought he was reading the *Bridlington Chronicle*, his brain was concentrating on the conversation behind him:

"Hope this gale drops, Sam. It's getting harder and harder to feed the kids. We need to be at sea, not stuck here," Ben Jemison took a gulp of his ale.

"Aye, Ben. But it's not all bad news. I hear as how some stuff was landed t'other day. Kit Brown were last in before the storm. Some say as how he came round the Head and not from fishing grounds. Now, what would he be doing t'other side of the Head?" Sam Beckwith leaned closer to Ben as he spoke.

As Officer Hythe heard this, he became convinced that Kit Brown had been round the other side of the Head to bring home contraband hidden in the chalk caves at Flamborough's North Landing.

Officer Hythe shivered again but the knowledge that he may soon apprehend a smuggler warmed him inside. The noise of iron wheels on the cobbles startled him. He squeezed into the shadow of the doorway and waited.

A dark figure passed a few feet in front of Hythe, who held his breath in silence. The figure was hauling a short cart, on top of which were two barrels. As the man's back turned on Hythe, the customs man leaned out of his hiding place. He watched as the man and the cart approached another door. That door, Hythe knew, led into the warehouse where Kit Brown kept his supplies.

Hythe watched the figure open the warehouse door and drag the cart inside. Hythe crept across the yard and, with his back to the wall, sidled up to the doorway. A candle was lit in the warehouse and Hythe watched as the figure lifted the barrels from the cart. The barrels were thrust under a bench and an old sail used to cover them. The figure blew out the candle and dragged the cart into the yard. Hythe waited until the door was closed, then stepped forward.

"Evening, Mr Brown. Or should I say good morning at this time of night?" Officer Hythe's attitude was one of complete self-assurance. "Can I ask you what you've just hidden under the bench in your warehouse? I don't think you were packing your fish. Could it be something brought from the caves at Flamborough? Something . . ." he paused, relishing the word he was about to say: "Smuggled?"

"Morning, Officer Hythe. There's nothing here for you to be concerned about. I'm only storing supplies that are my own. Nothing sinister about that, is there?"

"Well, Mr Brown," said Officer Hythe, licking his pencil after opening his notebook. "You say those goods are yours. But the question to be answered is: Should they be yours? And, more to the point, has duty been paid on whatever those goods are?" Hythe stood four-square in front of Kit Brown.

"Sorry, Officer Hythe. Everything is above board in there. I'll show you if you like."

"That won't be necessary, Brown. I've made a note and I expect to see you in court." Hythe put away his notebook and pencil, stuffed them into his coat pocket, turned and strode away.

"Damn!" said Kit Brown.

Chapter 27

15 April 1894

"Christopher Brown, known as Kit Brown. I find you guilty of possessing rum which it is alleged you procured from a passing merchantman in exchange for water. We have heard that your attempt at hiding the contraband failed when, due to his commendable vigilance, Customs Officer Hythe followed you from the harbourside to your cottage at No.3 Spring Pump Slipway. Before I pass sentence, have you anything to say?"

Kit Brown glanced down at his boots, the gleam on the toes not echoed in his eyes. He looked at the magistrate and said: "Nothing to say, Your Honour."

"Fined five shillings!" The magistrate banged his gavel on the desk, and gestured to the police constable to move Kit away.

Kit shrugged and left the courtroom. As he passed along the corridor of Bridlington Court House, a door opened and a clerk gestured for Kit to join him.

As Kit walked into the room, another door opened and Clarence Hythe stepped through.

"Kit! Kit! Come in." He paused, stood to one side, and added: "Please."

Kit Brown went into the second office and his eyes widened in surprise when he found himself in front of Magistrate Parslow again.

"Kit! Mr Brown. Please come in."

"Now what?" Kit blustered, looking from one face to the other. "What's up?"

"Well . . ." started Officer Hythe, "We were wondering if . . ."

"What's going on?" Kit, his anger starting to rise, approached the magistrate.

"Well . . ." said the magistrate. "Look, we're sorry

about having to fine you, Kit, er Mr Brown, but once the case was started it was impossible to stop and we had to go through with it. Officer Hythe thought he'd caught a real smuggler, but he'd copped you. He regrets it now, don't you Hythe?"

Clarence Hythe blushed and mumbled: "Yes, sir. Sorry Kit. I was only doing my job."

"Yes, yes, yes," said the magistrate. "So was I. But what we wondered was . . ." Magistrate Parslow seemed unsure of his words and looked towards Hythe.

"What we wondered was that the next time you do get hold of some more rum, you might let us know." Hythe blurted out the words and gulped, looking to Parslow for support.

"So, let me get this straight, gentlemen. You," Kit gestured at Hythe, "you arrest me and drag me to court. You," he said, pointing into the magistrate's face, "fine me five bob, then have the nerve to ask me for rum. Well, gentlemen, I might have been caught with a barrel of rum to sell to help feed my bairns. But it were gained by fair barter and exchange on the high seas, it weren't stolen, revenues had been paid, and I'll not help you two to take advantage of me. Both of you can well afford to buy the rum you need. Good day!"

Kit Brown turned, marched straight out of the office, down the corridor and into the street, where his smile spread, before bursting into a chuckle.

As he walked in the spring sunshine, Kit said to himself: "Well, Kit lad, it's not just the lifeboat service that has some peculiar goings-on."

Chapter 28

20 April 1894

Kit Brown glanced again at the horizon. He knew that the dark clouds looming in the north could either disappear as the sun rose higher or continue to mass and bring a storm.

In their coble *Elizabeth*, Kit and his two sons Fred and Frank had been tending to their long lines since dawn. They had laid their lines from east to west at the seaward side of the Smithwick Sands, where they expected to reap a good reward of codling.

Kit knew that on his previous trip he had made good money when he landed five baskets at Crane Wharf on Bridlington harbour.

The cloud had not changed since he last looked and he bent his back to attend to the lines. Fred leant back in the stern of the boat, his arm along the tiller. The sail hung loosely from the mast, and Frank wandered round the boat checking the rigging.

Another hour passed, with little conversation between father and sons. All three concentrated on their tasks, all three checking the crests of waves, the swell, the clouds, the strength of the wind and the hiss of the water as it ran down the side of the coble.

Kit looked north again. "Cloud's building, Fred. We might have to go in early."

"Not again, Dad! We'll never make a fortune if we don't catch as much as we can." Fred leant forward to shout across to his father. "I reckon we'll be all right," Fred continued and leant back again.

"Fat lot you know, Fred. That cloud's definitely building and if you look at the waves you'll see they're higher than they were a couple of minutes ago. There'll be a storm soon. Another hour and that'll be that."

Kit threw more line overboard until all was cast.

"Dad," started Frank. "Are we off to be safe out here if there's a storm?"

"Aye, lad. There's nowt to fear on the sea if you know what you're doing and if you go home before it's too bad. The measure of a sailor's skill is when to stop fighting the sea. Fight too long and she'll have you. You'll be so involved in the fight, you'll overlook the fact that you shouldn't being fighting but fleeing." Kit went to the prow of the boat and peered over at the bow wave.

"Aye, sea's running faster now. Anchor's reet tight. Tops of waves are breaking into spray. Bad sign that. We need to fetch the lines in soon." Kit followed Frank round the boat and tightened the lines to the sail. He looked up at the pennant on top of the mast. The triangular flag was beating a swift tattoo in the wind.

Kit wet his forefinger and held it out over the water. "Right, lads, let's get them lines in. We're off back."

"But Dad," shouted Fred, "You'll have nowt on them last lines. We won't make much brass if we go now. Let's hang on a bit longer. Half an hour."

"Fred, listen to me. We go now! Wind's getting up and look at them clouds. They're much nearer."

Fred tied a rope round the tiller and left the stern of the coble to help pull in the lines. Fred pulled the rope inboard and started to coil it at his feet. As a fish came over the side Fred unhooked it and flung it straight into a basket in the centre of the boat. He looped more rope and threw another fish. With his experienced rhythm, Fred continued to throw fish for the next quarter of an hour. When the end of the line was reached, he looped the rope on the growing pile.

Kit leant on the tiller and the coble scudded to another cork float. Fred started dragging the line aboard and once again fish after fish were cast into the baskets.

The clouds loomed directly overhead and the wind became colder. The sky was suddenly lit up by a flash of lightning followed immediately by a crack of thunder.

Within seconds rain poured into the coble, drenching the three fishermen.

"We have to make a run for it," shouted Kit, and turned the tiller for home.

After a little while Kit could see waves crashing onto Smithwick Sands. Breakers were pounding the sands throwing spray at least over the height of the coble's pennant.

"We'll not get past that lot, lads. Make for deep water. The storm will be over soon. It's a flash in the pan. If we stand off, we'll get through the Flamborough channel in a couple of hours I'm sure." Kit turned the coble so it faced the oncoming tide.

Kit ordered his sons to reef the sail while he struggled to keep the boat on the right heading. With less sail Kit knew he could keep *Elizabeth* away from the sandbank. He tacked back and forth over a small area of sea, flinging the tiller first one way, then the other. Fred and Frank untied and tied the ropes at their father's instruction. But despite all their efforts, the coble was gradually moving towards the sandbank. Kit looked over his shoulder and the waves were much closer. "Look, lads, we're going to have to make a run for it. I'm going for the Flamborough channel. It's going to be rough, very rough. Watch out for yourselves."

Kit swung the tiller and the coble forced its way along the line of breaking waves, heaving up and down as rollers passed under it. An occasional wave hurled spray into the boat, drenching the three men again. Fish and baskets slid along the bottom of the boat before crashing into the planks of the sides. Then they sloshed to the stern, crashing into the legs of the struggling men. The wind howled through the rigging and the pennant flapped even more furiously. Gradually the waves crashing on the bank eased as the water deepened and after a few more minutes the coble was out of danger.

Kit pushed the tiller and *Elizabeth*'s prow turned towards harbour. To starboard the grass-topped white chalk of Flamborough Cliffs towered over the boat and the rollers crashed onto the rocks. With the gale behind them, the coble sped before the waves, until Kit could make out the tower of Priory Church on the horizon. The clouds were still heavy overhead but to the west the sun blazed, casting hard shadows.

Fred looked at the church and remembered the Sunday School lesson of the legend of St John of Bridlington, who had helped five fishermen in distress by walking on the water to lead their vessel to safety. Fred asked God to be on his side every day he went to sea.

Chapter 29

30 May 1894

"Wow! Why haven't you shown us it before?" Billy Sawyer held Fred Brown's silver medal and gazed at it with eyes gleaming. "What you off to do with it?"

"Dunno. But stop shouting about it. My Dad'll play hell with me if he knows. I'm not supposed to bring it out." Fred took the medal back, breathed on it, rubbed it on the front of his gansey, and dropped it back in his pocket.

"Did you get any brass?" another youth asked.

"Oh, aye. I got a share-out of the money that was collected in Nottingham and Manchester. But my Dad's put it in the bank and I can't have it yet." Fred's face was downcast as he explained. "He says I'd only waste it down the *Crown & Anchor*."

Billy Sawyer said: "But there must be some way of making a bob or two from you having a medal. I mean, for life-saving, and all."

Fred, Billy, Frank and the others stopped to ponder the question.

As they puzzled, visitors passed them as they strolled in the May air.

A well-dressed couple walked towards the group of lads, then, giving them a wide berth, passed them by. The youths watched them promenade down the pier, the man's walking stick tap-tapping alongside him.

Fifty yards from the boys, the man's step faltered, he stumbled and his stick hit the low wall and fell into the harbour.

His cry of alarm alerted the boys and they ran up to him.

"What's up, mister?" said Fred, the other boys crowding round him.

"My stick! My lovely stick! It's gone! Over there!" He

pointed into the water sloshing in the corner of the harbour wall.

His companion cried: "And it's got a silver handle. Real silver!"

Fred Brown rubbed his hands together and, after a quick glance at his pals, said: "Well, it's lucky I'm here. My name's Fred Brown." And with that he dived over the harbour wall into the water.

"Aye," said Billy. "That's Fred Brown, he's a medal winner you know."

They all leaned over the wall and watched as Fred appeared spluttering and coughing with the walking stick in his raised hand.

"Hoorah!" shouted the man as his companion clapped her hands in thanks.

Fred Brown clambered up the steps to the pier top, shook himself, and offered the walking stick to the man.

"Thank you, thank you," the visitor said, looking at boys in turn. "How can I repay you?"

Each boy held out an outstretched palm.

"Ah, yes!" he said, and fumbled in his pockets. "Yes, for the hero, sixpence; and for his friends, a penny each."

The boys all nodded their thanks and watched as the couple returned to the pier steps to leave the pier.

The boys looked at the coins in their palms. Fred said: "That's one way of making some money. Rescuing things."

"But that got us a penny. We want some real money. More sixpences." Billy paused, and then grinned. "What if someone fell in, that'd do it."

"That's it!" exclaimed Fred. "No-one'll fall in very often though. But here's an idea." He gestured for the group of lads to come closer. "What about if I dived in to rescue somebody in the water, then got him out. The rest of you could say 'Fancy being rescued by Fred Brown. He's a medal winner, you know.' Then I bet you anything the visitors would cough up." Fred looked round at the group and beamed.

Frank Brown, always eager to be involved, piped up: "But who are you going to save?"

Fred put an arm around Frank's shoulder and said: "That's where you come in."

Frank's eyes look alarmed: "Oh?"

"Aye," said Fred. "You're eleven now and one of the gang, so what we do is this. You lot walk along north pier, then start pushing and shoving each other in fun, then Frank falls into the harbour. Then I rescue him. Easy!"

"But where will you be, Fred?" Frank asked, alarmed at the prospect.

"On the landing steps by Crane Wharf. I'll see you fall in, you lot shout that someone's in the water, I dive in, swim over to you and haul you out. They'll fall for it. You'll get tanners by the handful, I bet. You'll all be shouting your heads off on the pier and a crowd will gather there. I'll drag Frank back to Crane Wharf and there'll be dozens of folk there, and all. If we do that a couple of times a day, we'll make, er, well, lots of money."

"When you off to do it, Fred?" Billy Sawyer asked.

"There's a few folk about. Let's do it now!" said Fred, hopping up and down in excitement.

"What? Now?" A look of fright crossed Frank's face.

"Yes! Now! Come on! Right, I'm off to sit on the steps, you lot go to north pier and push him in." Fred turned to look at Frank. "You'll be all right. You can swim . . . a bit. But I'll be there in no time to save you. Let's go!"

The handful of visitors who happened to be in Bridlington in early May were not in the least surprised to see several youngsters jostling and pushing each other on the north pier. They looked with understanding as two of them started to shove each other more strongly. But they were alarmed when one youth fell over the harbour wall into the harbour. They dashed to the edge of the pier to see the youth floundering in shallow water. He was kicking his legs and flailing his arms and shouting at the top of his voice: "Help! Help! I can't swim!"

Then one onlooker shouted: "Look!" and all eyes turned to watch as a young man on steps on Crane Wharf leapt to his feet and tore off his jacket and boots. The visitors clasped their hands to their mouths in astonishment as the young man plunged into the water. He swam strongly towards the floundering youth and in a few strokes had reached him.

He grabbed the scruff of the youth's collar and hauled him back to Crane Wharf steps. Within a few minutes the incident was over, both youth and boy bedraggled and soaked. As they clung to each other, the other boys shouted: "Fancy that! He was saved by Fred Brown. He's a medal winner you know!"

Visitors opened their purses and pressed coins into willing hands as the story of Fred Brown's heroics fled round the harbour.

Some time later, at the end of north pier, the group of youngsters sat on the stone wall and counted their takings. There were several sixpences, many threepenny bits, handfuls of copper, but best of all, after two shilling pieces, was a sparkling sovereign.

"Right," said Fred. "I'll have the sovereign because it was my idea and I did the life-saving stunt."

"No," said Billy Sawyer. "No, Frank should get the sovereign because he could have drowned. You knew what you were doing. He didn't." Others of the group nodded.

"Just a minute," said Fred, "I say I should have the sovereign, and that's that!" He snatched at the coin, just as Frank reached for it as well. In seconds, both were scrapping and tussling for the coin. They rolled around on the pier bumping into legs and the wall.

They rolled as far as the edge of the pier, and struggled to get their footing. But the momentum of their bodies made them unbalanced and with a shout they both fell over the side. There was a double splash as they hit the water, and the group of youths leaned over to see them floundering. The water was deeper at this end of the pier, but both started to swim strongly across to the south pier, where the steps were nearer.

The brothers climbed the steps to the south pier, water flooding from their clothes. They shook their heads at the same time and both winced as the cold water hit their faces. They stamped their feet to rid their boots of water.

"Have you got that sovereign, Frank?" Fred demanded, holding out his palm.

"No! You had it!" Frank showed both his palms to Fred.

"Bloody hell!" said Fred. "That means we've lost it in t'water. You silly beggar!" Fred turned to Frank and gave him a push.

"Don't start again, Fred," Frank said as he moved away.

"Well, you've lost me that sovereign," Fred argued.

"No, you lost it, I reckon," Frank said.

The brothers trudged the length of south pier to Gummer's Wharf, crossed the width of the harbour, passed the Sailors' Bethel and into Queen Street. They trudged down Spring Pump Slipway until they came to their cottage.

Just as they neared the front door, their father saw them from his warehouse. He came over to them and asked: "What the hell have you two been doing?"

"Well . . ." said Fred.

"Well . . ." said Frank.

"Don't tell me. You've been fighting again."

"Not really, Dad. We fell in the harbour."

"Oh? You fell in the harbour. Just like that? Am I going to get an explanation?" Kit stood with hands on hips, waiting.

The boys both spoke together and Kit attempted to make sense of it all. He said: "Well, I reckon you deserve to lose that sovereign, much as we could have done with it. That's more than your mother gets for a week's work at the laundry. Perhaps it'll teach you not to be greedy." He

111

paused, then asked: "Is that all you got? Just that sovereign?"

"Oh, no, Dad. We got loads more," Fred started, while Frank interrupted with "There must have been another ten bob altogether."

"All right, then. Where is it?"

"That Billy Sawyer was counting it with us. He'll have it," Fred said.

"And will he tell you exactly how much you should have had?" asked Kit. "No? So you have no idea how much you had, and no idea how much he should give you? I don't know. What on earth am I going to do with you, Fred? You should be looking after your brother, keeping him out of bother. Good grief, lad, you're seventeen now. Will you ever grow up?"

Chapter 30

8 June 1894

"Frank, I've got a job for you." Kit Brown shouted up the stairs to rouse his son.

In his warehouse, Kit picked up the yoke he had made. About four feet in length, the yoke was shaped to sit on the shoulders. It had hooks dangling from chains hanging on the ends.

When Frank appeared, Kit put the yoke on his shoulders and stood back.

"There. That'll do."

"What's it for, Dad?" Frank moved his shoulders under the yoke so that it sat comfortably.

"It's so you can earn some brass, lad. You're always saying you want to help. Now's your chance." Kit Brown picked up two buckets and hung them on the hooks.

"Fill them buckets with water at the pump, then take them to Gladstone House on Esplanade. When you deliver the water they'll pay you. Bring the money back!"

"What? Carry two buckets of water all that way. I can't do that!" Frank lifted the yoke off his shoulders and put it on the floor.

"Yes, you can, lad. And you will. Now be off with you!"

Frank Brown picked up the yoke and replaced it on his shoulders.

He left the warehouse and clambered up the few steps to the pump. It seemed that everyone in the Quay had come to fill their buckets. As he waited, Frank read the stone again: "This spring was discovered by Benjamin Milne in 1811."

Frank pumped the handle until his two buckets were full of the pure spring water.

He bent his knees, put the yoke on his shoulders and

113

tried to stand. He forced his legs straight and found he could walk.

He staggered up the cobbled slope to Cliff Street. When the roadway had flattened out, he let the buckets down and repositioned the yoke.

Frank started his journey to the Esplanade. Within a few minutes he was on the seawall, and could see the whole of Bridlington Bay. Flamborough Head shone as the sun reflected off the white chalk, the sea was blue and to Frank it seemed a perfect summer's day.

He had only gone a few yards, when a couple of youths approached him.

"Where's thoo off with that watter, Frank?" asked Johnny Purvis.

"I'm off to Gladstone House on Esplanade. They'll pay me for this water when I get there." Frank smiled.

"Aye. But will you get a share of it? Or will it all go to your Dad?" Tom Jefferson asked.

"I might get a tanner, if my Dad's in a good mood when I get back. But I'm off now."

"We'll come with you," said Johnny.

"OK. But mind, I have to go straight there. My Dad'll be narked if I don't take him the brass straight away."

"Do you always do what your Dad tells you, Frank?" Tom asked.

"You don't know my Dad well enough to ask that! Of course I do. I've had the rope across my backside many a time. I played truant once. Teachers sent word that I hadn't been to school that morning. When my Dad asked if I'd been to school I said I had. So I got a few stripes of the rope, as he called it. Not for playing truant, but for lying to him."

"How much you going to get for the water, Frank?" asked Johnny.

"Dunno."

"So if you gave your Dad threepence less, he'd never know. Then we can have a penny each." Johnny rubbed his hands in anticipation.

"I'm going to buy some sweets with my penny," said Tom.

"Just a minute," said Frank, "I haven't agreed yet. But I reckon my Dad would never know, would he?" Frank looked from one face to the other for reassurance.

"No," they both replied.

When the three lads appeared at the front door of Gladstone House, the maid looked down her nose at them and commanded: "Go round the back; you can't come to the front door dressed like that!"

Frank said: "Please, miss, we don't know where to go. Show us!"

The maid indicated a passage at the side of the house.

The three boys trudged to the back door where they were met by a plump lady who asked: "Are you the lad from Brown?"

Frank looked at his companions and said: "Yes, I'm Frank Brown," to the accompaniment of nodding heads.

"Right, carry that water in here," the cook said, and she pointed at a large tank, "and pour it in there."

Frank lowered his yoke and the buckets were taken by Billy and Tom and the water poured into a large panchin.

"Thank you, boys. Would you like a cake?" the cook asked, indicating a plate full of buns.

"Yes, please," the boys said together.

"Get one each while I fetch the money," the cook said, and left the room.

As the boys were licking the last crumbs from their fingers, the cook returned and said: "Which one of you is going to take the money?"

"I'd better have that," said Frank, holding out his palm. "I've to give it to my Dad."

The cook counted out four silver threepenny pieces into his hand. "There's a shilling. Now off with you." She waved her hand to shoo them away.

The boys were soon walking back along the seawall towards the harbour. Tom said: "Give us our penny, Frank. You said you would."

Tom and Johnny held out their hands and Frank looked at them both before saying: "But I've only got threepenny pieces. I'll have to get pennies somewhere."

"Buy some sweets. Then we'll get change. Just get a pennorth then me and Tom can have our penny," said Johnny.

"Hang on a minute," said Frank. "Who gets the sweets?"

"You do," replied Johnny. "You get a pennorth of sweets and we get a penny. That's fair."

"But why can't you have the goodies and me have a penny?" asked Frank.

"Because we have to have the same pay," said Tom. "One penny. That's what was agreed." And he looked at Johnny.

"Aye," said Johnny. "A penny each, that's what you said."

"Come on then," said Frank, his voice full of resignation.

Frank bought the pennorth of sweets and put them in his pocket. He handed over a penny to Tom and Johnny.

"Give us a humbug, Frank," commanded Tom.

"And I'll have one and all," added Johnny.

Without thinking, Frank handed each a single sweet.

"Hey, just a minute. You're getting more than me. That's not fair," Frank started to shout.

"We don't care, Frank Brown. Take your money to your Dad." Tom and Johnny ran off down Garrison Street, laughing.

Frank Brown trudged home, the yoke jangling along the road as he dragged it behind him.

When he arrived at the warehouse, he put the yoke on the bench, and went indoors to take the money to his father.

"I've got the money, Dad!" he called.

His father appeared and asked: "How much did you get?"

Frank shifted his feet uneasily. "Well," he started.

116

"Yes?" asked his father.

"Ninepence." Frank's voice was subdued as he tried to look his father in the eye and held out the money in his palm.

"Ninepence? Ninepence? The thieving swindling beggar. Ninepence?" Kit Brown stomped around the warehouse, his face red with anger.

"What's up, Dad?" Frank said, taking a step towards the door, the words thieving and swindling showing him something he wished he wasn't.

"That bloke promised me a shilling. And he sends my lad back with ninepence. I'll give him ninepence." Kit Brown reached for his jacket.

"Dad . . ." said Frank, voice filled with trepidation.

"What?" Kit stopped at the door.

Frank remembered the rope across his backside for lying before.

"He did give me a shilling. But Tom and Johnny helped me and I gave them a penny each. And I bought a pennorth of sweets with my share." Frank hung his head, after gabbling his explanation.

"Your share? Your share? It was all going to be yours. I thought you'd earned it, lugging all that water up to Gladstone House."

Frank looked at his father with astonishment. "What, all for me? The whole shilling?"

"Yes, Frank. The whole shilling. So to teach you a lesson I shall keep half and you can have this threepenny piece. Just remember, Frank, don't try and outsmart your father. He's been around too long for that."

"Thanks, Dad. Is there anything I can do for you?" Frank's voice was eager.

"Nay, lad. I'm off to a meeting of the lifeboat committee in an hour and I'm away in for my tea. Coming?"

"Aye," said Frank, caressing the money in his pocket but wishing he hadn't listened to Tom and Johnny.

Chapter 31

21 June 1894

"Dad! Dad! I've had an idea!" Fred Brown burst into the warehouse, where his father was preparing salt beef.

"Oh, yes, Fred. And what idea's this then? Is it better than that one where you threw our Frank into the harbour?"

"I heard there were some special trains coming in this weekend," Fred's voice was full of excitement.

"So?" asked Kit.

"Well, all the visitors will walk down Hilderthorpe Road straight to the seawalls and harbour." Fred's arms flailed as he emphasised the location of these attractions.

Kit Brown stopped work and looked up at Fred. "So what?"

"Well, Dad, you're always on at me to be mature so I checked the tide and it will be full at two o'clock on Saturday afternoon."

Kit Brown bent over the barrels of meat. "What are you getting at Fred?"

"Well, why don't we .. ? Why can't we .. ?"

"Get on with it, lad!" Kit shouted.

"Why don't we take them out on the *Elizabeth*?"

"Take who out on *Elizabeth*?" Kit stopped again with a puzzled look on his face.

"The holidaymakers, Dad, the holidaymakers. They've come to Brid for a change. So let's give 'em one. Let's take them out into the Bay for a sail." Fred straightened up and threw out his chest. "It's a good idea, isn't it? We'd make a bob or two, wouldn't we?"

"What about our fishing?" Kit asked.

"Bugger fishing, Dad. We don't do owt in summer anyway. I'm thinking of making more money than the few coppers we get for our fish. Let others fish. We'll

118

make money from the visitors. No-one else has thought of it yet. Let's be the first."

"Well," said Kit slowly. "It might work."

"It would work, Dad. I'm sure of it. Just think. Let's say we got twenty people . . ."

"Twenty!" Kit Brown dropped a side of beef into a barrel in his surprise.

"Well, then, ten," Fred Brown said. "There's plenty of room in the *Elizabeth*. Three of us: me chatting to the folk and collecting their brass and you and somebody else sailing the boat, one on the sail, the other on the tiller." Fred numbered the tasks on his fingers.

He started again: "Let's say we charge them threepence apiece . . ."

"Threepence? Are you out of your mind? They won't pay that!" Kit shook his head.

"Well, tuppence then. Tuppence a trip. Sounds good does that. Tuppence a trip." Fred shouted the last words as though he was on the harbour walls.

"Yes, Dad. Tuppence a trip. That's one and eightpence every time we go out. We only need to be out quarter of an hour, then come back. Say three trips an hour. That's five shillings an hour. Five shillings, Dad. Think of that. And how many hours could we do in summer? Eight? Nine? Ten? That's two pound ten shillings a day. And we could do it every day all through the summer. Dad, we could be rich after a year."

Fred's monologue came to a sudden end when he couldn't think of anything else to say.

"It sounds all very well," Kit said. "But what about wet weather, and gales, and low tide. What about them, Fred?" Kit shook his head again.

"But, Dad! If we're earning that kind of brass a few missing trips aren't going to matter, are they?"

There was silence for a few moments before Kit asked: "How much did you say we could get in a day, Fred?" Kit Brown looked carefully at his son.

"Two pounds ten shillings. Fancy, Dad. Two pounds

ten. We'd have to sell more fish than we could ever catch to make that." Fred started to rub his hands together as though he could see the pile of coins in front of him.

"Two pounds ten. But we'd have to share it with somebody else," Kit said. "But I bet Dick Purvis wouldn't mind helping out. Just to see if the idea works. I'll ask him."

"Shall I go for him, Dad? Now?" Fred made to leave the warehouse.

"Hang on, lad. Not so hasty. I haven't said we'll do it yet." Kit Brown put the last roll of beef into the barrel and banged a lid into place.

"So, Fred. How are you going to get folk to know about it?"

"Well, I reckon I'd stand by the boat at the landing stage, and shout. I could shout 'Anyone for sailing? Tuppence a trip. Sail into Bridlington Bay. Tuppence a trip.'

"Once a few got on and others had seen the boat full of holidaymakers more people would want to sail. I reckon they'd be queueing on a good day. And we can be first, Dad. Just think, something new in Brid and it was me who thought of it first." Fred filled his chest with pride and beamed at his father.

"All right, lad. I reckon as we ought to give it a try. You'd better pray for a fine day come Saturday." Kit hammered nails into the lid of his barrel.

Fred Brown strutted the length of the warehouse, shouting: "Anyone for sailing? Tuppence a trip."

"Anyone for sailing? Tuppence a trip." Fred Brown stood at the steps on north pier and shouted again. Further along the pier Kit was shouting the same message.

At the foot of the steps, eight holidaymakers clung to the sides of the the coble *Elizabeth* and gazed at the closeness of the waves. The water in the harbour rippled slowly down the side of the boat but to the people from Leeds, Halifax and Wakefield it was somewhat alarming as it was so close.

"Come on folks. Sail in the Bay. Only tuppence a trip."

A couple in their weekend best approached Fred and offered four pennies. "Thank you Sir, Madam," said Fred. "This way." He escorted the pair down the steps and helped them into the coble. When they were seated, Fred shouted up to Kit: "Let's go, Dad!"

Kit hurried down the steps and into the boat. He untied the rope keeping the coble secure, while Fred and Dick hoisted the sail and put the rudder in place.

Within a few minutes, *Elizabeth* was scudding across the bay, her rust-red sails filled with the breezes of early summer.

The bench in Kit Brown's warehouse looked more like a bank counter than a fisherman's workplace.

Arranged on its surface were piles of coins. There were half-pennies piled in twelves, pennies in twelves, three-penny pieces in fours, and a scattering of sixpences and shillings. And, on its own, at the end of the bench, a half crown.

On the last trip of the day, Kit had been offered the silver coin when six men in their Saturday suits asked to be taken into the Bay. Kit took the coin and gave the man his change, a handful of small silver. As the men sat on the wooden seats of the coble, Kit looked at the coin again. "Half a crown," he murmured. He rubbed it between his thumb and forefinger. It felt thick, solid and safe.

Their first day in Bridlington harbour operating as pleasure boat operators had brought a total of one pound eight shillings and four pence.

Kit looked at the money again.

"Well, Dick. What does tha think?"

"Kit, it looks like your lad has had a good idea at last. I like it and we should do it again next weekend. It's a damn sight easier than fishing."

He and Kit took out five shillings for the boat, two shillings for Fred, and took three shillings and sixpence each.

"What'll you do with the rest?" Dick asked.

"I've thought of that. I'm off to open a bank account. I shall see Mr Mortimer at Burlington Bank. They'll look after it for me. Then I'll perhaps buy a bigger boat."

"By heck, Kit, thou's off to make a name for thissen in Brid."

"'Appen," said Kit. "'Appen!"

Chapter 32

29 November 1897

He stood, resolute. His bulk stoppered the door through to the snug. The rain-slicked coat reflected the light from half-a-dozen spluttering oil lamps. The steady drip of water formed a small pool by his black-booted feet, then gradually grew to a puddle. The man's bronzed face peered at the men in the bar, one face at a time, reading whatever message he could.

Reaching barely five and a half feet in height, Thomas Atkin nevertheless looked every inch a mariner. His gaze was the result of years glaring through gales, storms, even tempests and monsoons. The blueness shone as if back lit by a huge incandescence, a blueness which had battled against wind and tide in Atlantic, Pacific, Indian and even the Arctic oceans.

His right hand, fingers twisted like twigs from a hawthorn tree, gripped his walking stick, a dark brown polished to a bright smoothness with hours of handling in long dull days ashore.

Despite his necessary use of a stick, Thomas stood firmly, a rigidity which had held against mutinous crews, rebellious mariners and intransigent masters.

On this day of all days, no-one would cross Atkin. He had an announcement to make which would pierce the very souls of the men downing their draughts of rum.

He flung the door shut. The slam penetrated the eager discussions among Bridlington's fishermen. A silence descended, broken only by the crash of a glass on the floor.

Atkin's fist pounded the counter as he bawled: "Our boat will not be launched. The National boat will take the call and we're not needed"

An instant hubbub chased the silence from the pub

and followed it outside where it fell upon the ears of wives, mothers, sons and daughters who had seen Atkin's purposeful strides a few minutes earlier.

In the snug of *The Albion*, one man stood up to face Atkin.

"Tell him, John!" came a shout from near the far wall. "You tell him we're going."

The standing man swung to face Atkin, his eyes looking down into the old man's face.

Atkin held out a restraining hand, holding it short of the man's chest. "Now lad, don't make things worse. Sit theeself down. We want no bother."

Atkin shook himself and a flurry of droplets spun to the floor. He removed his souwester and his shock of pure white hair was haloed round his head. He ran his fingers from his brow to the nape of his neck in a manner too gentle for such a bulky man.

"I've looked at the tide, judged the wind and seen the sky. We'd never reach her, and even if we did we'd be in no shape to give help." Atkin used the 'we' even though he knew he would not be aboard the lifeboat. As secretary he had the power to say yes or no to a launch but his time at sea was nearly over. "I don't even think the National boat will launch."

John Jemison, the man who had sat down at Atkin's command, rose again. "Look, Atkin. The men think we ought to go. And as cox I agree. We have to try."

"Nay, lad. Trying's not enough. There's nowt to be gained by flogging yoursens to death for no good reason. I know the bay as well as any of you, better'n most, and I say it's impossible!"

"But that's what we're here for, ain't it?" A younger voice bellowed out what the majority of the men were thinking.

Another voice boomed from the men: "There's not much point in having a lifeboat if we don't go out when it's dangerous. There's sailors out there in a boat on the Smithwick. They'll be goners unless we get to them."

124

There was a chorus of "Aye!"

"You're not going to die uselessly." Atkin looked at each man's face briefly as though trying to impress his thoughts directly on the man's brain. "But if I allow you to launch that's what will happen. You're all good lads, every one of you, but I'd be failing in my duty if I let you launch only to drown yourselves." Atkin paused and straightened his back, his fists clenched and supporting him on the table.

"Another hour, and I'll look again." Atkin turned his back on the men, marched through the door and into the gathering storm.

Chapter 33

29 November 1897

He knew what he'd done as soon as he closed the lifeboat house door. The bolt was well greased and slid easily into place. That would hold them for a while. But, thought Captain Atkin, they were in a terrible mood out there. No-one likes being called a coward and although no-one had actually used the word, he knew that that's what would be implied by some.

Captain Atkin, his grey beard bristling as he ran his twisted right hand through it, could hear the shouts of the fishermen outside.

"Open this damned door, Atkin!" It was louder than the general hubbub. And he recognised it as being Fred Brown's.

"Hasn't Kit Brown controlled that son of his yet?" he muttered as he backed to the rear of the lifeboat house, a wooden extension to the Workingmen's Club. He gazed at the *Seagull*.

Many years had passed since he took on the onerous task of lifeboat secretary and he'd faced many problems in that time. Today, however, he had made a difficult choice. He'd told them, coxon and crew of the lifeboat, not to launch.

He'd heard all the cries of fishermen advising him to let them go, that they were lifeboatmen and needed to go. That lives would be lost.

Captain Atkin knew they would never make it. And told them so. "The seas are too high, them breakers are huge, the wind's in the wrong direction, the tide's against you." But still they had hollered and swore and demanded to launch.

Even Coxon Jemison paid no heed to Atkin's superior knowledge. Jemison shouted: "I'm an experienced fisherman in these waters and I reckon we should get out there and save the crew."

Atkin replied: "I've spent twenty years on the oceans of the world, I've sailed the Bay of Biscay, the Roaring Forties, the Capes, even through the Timor Straits. I've been to the Arctic and the Antarctic. What I don't know about the sea don't matter a damn. But what I do know is that it's near suicide to launch the *Seagull*."

"Open up Atkin, or we're coming in!" Once again Brown's voice broke through the din. The shout was accompanied by thumping and hammering on the door, which rattled and shook.

"I'm not launching the boat. Go home!" Atkin shouted in reply. "It's not a Bridlington job. It's one for them at Flamborough! Anyway, the National will go before us."

"Rubbish! Open up!"

Captain Atkin went to the door and slid back the lock. "Hang on then!" he shouted.

But as his fingers felt the cold of the steel, the door bowed inwards. With a huge crash, it sprang open and smashed into the wall. It missed Atkin by inches. He looked into the night. A flickering torch splashed light on to angry faces. Standing before him were men he knew well. But their manner was belligerent and aggressive.

"I can see you! Jemison! Jewitt! Creaser! Crawford! Brown! Go home! I'm not giving the boat to you lot!"

"We're tekkin the *Seagull*, Atkin," Fred Brown barked and pushed a hand at Atkin's chest.

"Over my dead body, Brown." Atkin puffed out his chest and stood his ground.

Brown's eyes were fixed on Atkin's. "Aye, man, and that could be arranged." For only the second time in his life had Atkin realised he was being faced by a man with a stronger will than his own.

"Tek her then. I wash my hands of yer. You'll probably wreck the boat and all drown into the bargain." Atkin took two steps back from Fred and waved his ruined hand at the vessel.

"'Appen we will," said Fred, "but at least we'll have tried." He turned to the crowd of men. "Come on, lads. There's no trouble here."

Atkin stood against the wall, shaking his head slowly, watching as a dozen men seethed past him. They grabbed lifejackets and oars, slung them aboard the wooden boat, then started to heave on the ropes.

The *Seagull* had not been moved for months and the carriage she was sitting on was stiff with rust. The men heaved and pushed. More men poured into the building until it seemed to Atkin that it was a human ant hill. He remembered seeing red ants in Africa as he watched the men run to and fro trying to find a place to push.

Fred's voice rang out once again. "Heave, lads, heave!" Slowly the wheels turned. *Seagull* was hauled into the night to be assailed by wind and snow.

Fred Brown turned to Atkin. "You should be with us, Captain."

"Nay, lad." Atkin shook his head with sorrow. "You've brought all this on yersens. Tomorrow will show how stubborn and stupid you were."

"'Appen," said Fred, turning away, "but at least I'll know I weren't a coward."

Men hauled the boat outside, just as the horses arrived from their field. The men shackled the horses into the harness and the animals, with a sharp slap on their flanks, started to haul the carriage and boat down Cliff Street.

Men were piling into the boat, tying their cork jackets around their midriffs. As they were hauled onto the seafront, the men faced the full fury of the storm.

The horses and carriage careered down the slipway, the wheels slipping on the snow, the launch crew hauling on ropes to provide braking.

By this time, townsfolk had learned that the lifeboats may be launched, and crowds had closed their shutters, making for the harbour. By the time the *Seagull*'s carriage was on the sands, hundreds of people, old men, women and children, were swarming around the scene. Many were urging the horses to greater effort, others were pushing the carriage, while more were offering advice to the crew.

Fred gazed at the throng. "Hell, Jack, that's quite a turn-out tonight," said Fred, leaning close to Jack's ear to make sure he heard him.

"Aye, lad, they're always here. Don't know what makes them do it."

"Maybe so. And I don't really know what makes us do this either!"

A sudden roar from the crowd swelled and the men on the lifeboat leaned over the side to find out what was happening.

Captain Atkin strode up to the side of the boat. "You're not launching."

"We're all ready to go. What's stopping us?" Fred shouted at him.

"I've heard from Flamborough. The boat's sunk. She's gone. Get that boat back in the house." Atkin turned on his heel and walked away.

"Bloody hell," said Fred. "What on earth will Dad say?"

Chapter 34

25 March 1898

"Kit! Kit!" Dick Purvis burst into Kit's warehouse, his face red with exertion. "They're launching the lifeboats!"

"I've not heard the maroons," Kit looked up as he closed another barrel of fish.

"No! It's the men! They've taken the *Seagull* from the boathouse again. Atkin's going barmy!"

Kit reached for his hat, stuck it over his thinning grey hair, and went to the door.

"So, what happened?"

"Well," said Dick. "Apparently some of the young men have taken the *Seagull* up to the Cut to launch her. And the National crew have taken their boat, too."

"But, why?" asked Kit.

"There's a ship showing a flag. I reckon it's a call for a pilot but those young hotheads reckon it's a call for help. Your lad's there, you know."

"What? Our Fred?" Kit asked.

"Yes, your Fred, and all his mates. I hear they bashed the door in with a coble's mast because Atkin and the coxswains wouldn't give permission."

"Oh, God! What have they taken *Seagull* for? She's in no state for a gale. We'll need ropes. Take these coils, Dick, I'll get more. God! The last thing we need is another lifeboat fiasco."

The two men slung the coils of rope over the shoulders and rushed to the harbour wall.

There was no sign of activity, only the restless sea in the harbour, but they could both see waves crashing into the wall in the corner of south pier and the road.

"Come on, Dick!" Kit started to hurry up Harbour Road towards the north pier. Here they looked along the seawall, and in the distance they could just make out two separate groups of men and flashes of white paint of the lifeboats.

Puffing and panting as they went, Kit and Dick looked out to sea. The waves were crashing into the seawall and spray was being thrown across the road into the facing buildings. The wind howled and they could feel sleet and snow in the wetness of the wind.

At Trinity Cut, a crowd of men surrounded the RNLI lifeboat, urging the crew to get aboard.

The coxswain shouted: "We can't go yet, the Captain hasn't given permission!"

"Bugger Atkin!" shouted a voice in the crowd. "Get that boat launched!"

"No. We can't! Not until we get the all clear. Atkin needs to give permission!"

"Well, where is he then?"

"He'll be making his mind up, won't he? There's a lot to think about." The coxswain tried to control the men but they were in no mood for that.

"Look out, here's Atkin!" shouted a voice, and the crowd parted as Captain Atkin pushed his way through.

"You're not launching this boat. Not yet, anyway!"

"And why not, Atkin?" came an angry shout.

"Because I say so, that's why. I'm Lifeboat Secretary and I say it's too dangerous to launch now. Wait until the tide's off the wall, about an hour. That boat will still be out there. We'll go in an hour!"

Captain Atkin turned his back on the men round the boat and disappeared into the crowd.

"Right, that's it, then. We're not going," the coxswain turned to the men. "Let's wait."

Men and women surged round the boat, and there were calls for the boat to launch, others for the men to hang on.

Chapter 35

25 March 1898

Turning his back on his friends was hard for Kit Brown, but he knew he had to leave them. With a final nod to Dick Purvis and the others nearby, Kit slung his two coils of rope across his shoulders again, and pushed through the crowd surrounding the RNLI boat.

After his previous exertions, Kit was weary and he gasped as he trudged along the seawall from Trinity Cut towards Sands Lane. The wind tore his breath away and the spray coming over the wall stung his eyes. He peered through the storm and he could make out a crowd at the top of the slipway.

As he approached, men turned towards him then whispered: "It's Kit Brown. He'll know what to do."

Kit approached the stern of the *Seagull* and shouted up to Tom Hutchinson, the coxswain: "Don't go! It's far too dangerous!"

"We're waiting for Atkin to give us the word," Tom called back.

"OK!" said Kit, and motioned for Tom to come down to the slipway. Kit watched as the man lowered himself over the side of the lifeboat and drop to the ground.

"Look!" said Kit, "There's no need to launch yet anyway. That boat is only showing a flag for a pilot. It's not a distress flag. If we wait an hour the tide will be off the wall, and then you'll have the whole beach to come back to."

"But the men want to go, Kit. Their minds are made up. They don't want to wait for Atkin." Tom Hutchinson paused. "In case he doesn't let them go again. There'd be hell on then, you'll see."

"Well, Atkin's in charge. It's down to him. He's answerable to the committee," Kit tried to explain.

"Bugger the committee, and bugger Atkin." A young face peered from the *Seagull*. "Tell them, Dad. You tell them to let us go," said Fred Brown.

"What the hell are you doing on there?" Kit's voice was raised in anger at the sight of his son.

"I'm doing my bit, that's all. They needed a crew so I volunteered," Fred said.

"Who authorised this? Who let Fred get in the boat?" Kit turned round to the crowd, searching every face.

"Well, Kit, he volunteered, and we need the men," Tom Hutchinson said, hunching his shoulders in apology.

"But if Atkin doesn't give you permission, you're not likely to launch. You could have waited for a more experienced crew," Kit shouted at the assembled men and women.

"Come on, let's go!" shouted Fred Brown. "There's no point in having a lifeboat if it doesn't go out when it's needed," and the other young men in the crew shouted: "Aye!"

"So how long do we have to wait? Where's Atkin? He's never around when you want him! Bloody typical!" Fred shouted down to his father.

Tom Hutchinson shook his head, and turned to Kit. "I'm standing down. I'm not having the prospect of launching without permission on my head." He raised his voice and the crowd turned towards him. "I'll not be coxswain with this lot!" He turned his back on the boat and the crew.

"Right, then! I'll do it. I've skippered the boat before." An older man pushed his way to the front and stood in front of the coxswain.

"I wash my hands of this." Hutchinson glowered at the crowd, and went back towards the harbour, a lonely figure hunched in his misery, passing a man running towards the lifeboat.

"They've launched the National boat!" The man was red with effort and his clothing dripped with water from the crashing seas.

The crowd became more and more agitated. Men were shouting and women screaming at each other – and their men.

"What shall we do?" a voice shouted from the boat.

"Get that boat in the water. What's the matter with you? Bloody lifeboatmen. You're all cowards!" A slurred voice came from the back of the crowd.

The crowd was suddenly galvanised into action. Men swarmed around in the boat, taking up their oars ready for the moment the boat hit the water. Other men and many of the women hauled on ropes or pushed the carriage of the boat to move it from a standstill.

"Come on! Put your backs into it!" The slurred voice once again was louder than the generous buzz of noise from the crowd.

At last, the boat and carriage started to move down the slipway. Waves were pounding the seawall and water was surging up the slipway. The carriage stopped, caught on a chunk of chalk thrown up by the waves. A man ran to the front of the carriage and kicked at the stoppage. Once freed, the carriage trundled towards the sea.

Back on the seawall, Kit Brown watched with dismay. They hadn't listened to him. The crew had allowed themselves to be persuaded by a drunken voice, probably from a man who'd spent the day in a public house fortifying himself with rum.

He watched the lifeboat make its way through the rolling sea as it headed towards the stricken vessel. It crested one wave, then another, then a third.

Kit was about to make his way back to the harbour, when he saw an oar break away from the boat and hit the water. Kit shouted "Look out!" and the crowd surged forward towards the seawall.

Chapter 36

25 March 1898

Kit Brown was aghast when he realised what had happened. The *Seagull*'s oars had been smashed by the power of the waves and the lifeboat was being pushed back towards the seawall. Each successive wave brought the boat nearer disaster.

Broadside on, the boat took the full force of the tide and smashed into the stone. The crew were thrown off their feet as they struggled to stand. Ropes were thrown from the onlookers to straddle the craft and a crew member grabbed one tight and leaped overboard. He was hauled up the wall by many willing hands and he was able to scramble to safety.

Another great wave smashed the boat against the wall and many of the crew were pitched headlong into the ferocious sea. As they were thrown at the wall, one or two found a footing and clung on. Hands reached down to them, but the huge bible-back stone on top of the wall impeded their rescue.

The next wave swept them off the wall and carried them towards steps which on kinder days led down to the sand.

Kit Brown's anger at the sea welled up in him. He took the end of a rope and tied it round his waist. He shouted to those holding it: "Hang on to this rope for dear life!"

Kit took each step into the sea. When the sea fell away between waves, he advanced a further step then prepared himself for the onslaught of the water. The wave broke over him, forcing him to his knees, and then fell back. He took another step into the sea.

A fisherman was floundering in the waves. "Help me, Kit!" He recognised the voice and realised it was his cousin Christopher. Kit reached out to grab him by the

135

gansey and shouted "I've got you!" Chris reached for Kit's arm and they clung to each other.

"Haul us up! Haul away!" Kit screamed at those on the rope, and they were dragged towards the steps.

Kit found his footing and half carried his cousin up the steps to safety.

He turned to go down the steps again, just as Jack Creaser was hauling John Hopper to safety. "Well done, Jack!" Kit said, and Jack replied: "Your lad's still aboard!"

"Oh! God! No!" Kit charged down the steps and he reached the sand with the waters surging about his chest. He looked into the waves but could see no-one. A few feet away the *Seagull* was being pounded against the seawall.

Kit made his way back up the steps one by one as the breakers still covered him. He was half-way up the steps when a huge wave, far bigger than any before, swept over him. As he tumbled and rolled under the water, he felt the rope torn from his fingers. He surfaced, spluttering and coughing, to find the lifeboat looming over him. He reached for the ropes hanging from the boat and grabbed them with both hands. As he hung there, gasping and freezing, a face appeared over the side of the lifeboat.

Fred Brown saw his father in the water and shouted at him: "What the hell do you think you're doing?"

"I'm doing my best. I'm trying to save lives at sea. Get me aboard, Fred." Fred grabbed him, heaved and Kit managed to haul himself onto the *Seagull*.

The two men glared at each other. "What possessed you to launch? You knew it was too much for the boat. Why don't you ever listen to me?" Kit hollered above the crashing waves and howling wind.

Fred shouted back: "Because I wanted to do it my way for once. You always think you're right, don't you?"

"Well, I were right, weren't I? Now get a rope round yer, and jump, you daft bugger, jump!"

Fred grabbed one of the ropes still lying over the boat, tied it round himself. "Come on, Dad. I'll help you." Fred reached for a rope for his father, but another huge wave smashed into the boat. With a shout of alarm, Fred reached for his father's arm but was pitched into the sea.

Kit looked up at the men on the wall and could see hundreds of faces, white in the gloom, staring down at him. He shouted: "Help him!"

Kit found another rope, and tied it round his chest under his arms. He shouted "Pull me in!" Then the rope tightened. Another wave crashed into the lifeboat and Kit was thrown clear into the seething tide.

The icy water hit him in the face again and he gasped, trying to catch a breath. He reached for the rope above his head and tried to cling on.

The *Seagull* ground its way along the seawall losing planks, ropes and cork. As Kit was being hauled through the waves a broken oar from the *Seagull* hit Kit on the head and he saw stars.

In his mind he saw the face of his wife Mary, and murmured "Sorry, Mary," and he knew he could die.

Kit then realised that he was half out of the water and was being hauled up the face of the wall. He hung, water falling from his body back into the raging seas. He was pulled higher and higher up the wall, until his hands touched the bible-back. Other hands reached over for him and grasped his wrists. He knew those above him were struggling to hold him but he was unable to help. Any strength he had had been taken from him by the cold. Suddenly the rope was loose and Kit fell with a huge splash into the sea.

He was knocked over and over as the tide surged forward. The rope wrapped itself round his legs and he struggled to free himself.

As he surfaced, Kit saw someone near him and a pair of arms reached for him. "Here, Kit! Grab my arm!" Kit saw a face he recognised. "Help me, Alf! Help me!" Alfred Stephenson, the harbourmaster, hung on the end of a rope. He grasped Kit and the men clung together. Still gasping and spluttering, Kit held as tight as he could as they were hauled up the wall.

Once again the bible-back impeded the rescuers. Kit was exhausted, the freezing cold and strenuous efforts having drained his strength.

Alf held on for as long as he could but Kit's weight and the cold were too much. Stephenson shouted: "I can't hold him," and Kit fell back into the water, with a despairing shout of "Oh! help me! God help me!"

Through the spray Kit could just see Alf being lowered again. He reached out for him, but he hadn't the energy to swim to him. The last thing Kit saw was the line of faces staring down at him. As the waves closed over him for the last time, he heard Fred scream: "Daaaaaad!"

Chapter 37

29 March 1898

Breakfast was over in a sombre Brown household. Mary Brown's daughters and their husbands had gone to Prince Street to buy mourning clothes. Mary was alone in the Spring Pump Slipway cottage when Frank burst in.

"Mam! There's a naval officer outside. He's come about Dad."

He turned and watched as a tall man resplendent in naval uniform ducked his head to enter the room.

"Morning, Mrs Brown. I'm Lieutenant Smith and I'm here to arrange the funeral of Mr Brown."

"But he was never in the services," said Frank.

"He wasn't in the services, that's true. But before you were born, your father was a pilot for all the naval cutters that came into Bridlington Bay. He found them a safe anchor. So, for us, he was classed as a naval officer."

"I remember him doing that when you were just a nipper, Frank," Mary said, then turned to the officer: "You must do what you must do, young man." Mary Brown's voice was quiet and calm, and she looked about her as though not seeing anything.

"Are you going to use a gun carriage, then?" asked Frank.

"We'll sort all that out with your mother, and . . . is it Fred?" the officer asked.

"No, I'm Frank, Fred's my brother. He's down the harbour just now," Frank explained.

"Well, we'll look after things from now on. You know, you'll have to stop so many people coming to see him. This cottage is old, and there's hundreds of people outside wanting to pay their last respects. The floorboards may give way if there's too many at a time. Can you let only a handful in at once, Frank? And tell them I said so!"

"Aye, I'll do that for you," Frank replied, and there was eagerness in his voice.

Ten minutes later, Fred entered the room and the officer went through the details again. He went on: "I've come with half a dozen ratings. They'll carry the coffin."

"But my Dad's mates will want to do that. You can't keep them out of it!" Fred raised his voice.

"Well, we'll share the duties. I suggest that eight fishermen carry the coffin from the cottage up the hill to Cliff Street. Then we'll put the coffin on the hearse. Your mother has chosen that rather than a gun carriage. When we get to the church, my six ratings and a couple of coast-guards can carry him from the cemetery gates into the church. After the service, the fishermen can take him from there to the grave. I think that will satisfy everyone." The officer looked at Frank, Fred and Mary. All nodded.

"Good. Well if you'll excuse me, I'll go about my business." The officer stood up, collected his papers, and left the room.

Frank and Fred went to their mother and put an arm round her shoulders. "It'll be all right, Mam," Frank reassured his mother.

"Aye, Mam," Fred said. "It'll be all right. But, you know, I don't think I knew my Dad at all."

Chapter 38

5 April 1898

Bridlington awoke from its slumbers. One by one blinds were raised, people left their homes and opened their businesses. The baker's window was filled with fresh bread, while the butcher hung chickens and rabbits from hooks above the window and placed joints of beef, pork and lamb on display inside. The townsfolk began the struggle back to their everyday lives.

Fisherwomen gathered at their stalls along the harbour to sell the first fish caught after the funeral. Boys and girls meandered their way to school, and old men leaned over the pier walls to talk about the sea.

Fred Brown limped through the cottage door on Spring Pump Slipway to face a future without the guiding hand of his father, and knowing that he was now the man of the family. The face of Bridlington looked the same, but Fred knew everyone and everything would be different from this day on.

He resolved that from that morning he would do all he could to support the new lifeboat service in Bridlington. That was something he could do to make amends. He'd been at the meeting of the Sailors' and Workingmen's Club two days earlier when it was decided that it should no longer support a private lifeboat. Fred realised it was the end of an era, and that future Bridlington lifeboats would be the sole responsibility of the Royal National Lifeboat Institution. He was determined to be part of the crew, as soon as he could discard his crutches, and his legs had healed.

He stepped onto the cobbles, with Frank close behind, and the brothers made their way up the slope to Cliff Street. They walked in silence towards the sea, nodding quiet greetings to those who passed. At the top of north pier, they turned into Garrison Street and slowly approached Fort Hall.

On its carriage outside the hall, the wreck of the *Seagull* was a reminder to everyone of what had happened eleven days before. Two gaping holes in the planks where the vessel had smashed into the seawall were obvious to all. Fred had agreed with the Club decision to use the *Seagull* to collect money for the Kit Brown Fund and Robert Pickering's family. Robert's legs were crushed during the loss of the *Seagull*. The lifeboat was then to be cut up and the pieces sold to raise even more money.

Fred and Frank walked round the boat and Fred shuddered as he remembered those last few moments before he was rescued. He visualised his father's face looking up at him from the raging sea. He flexed his muscles as he relived the effort of hauling him aboard. His throbbing knees were a constant reminder of how the sea battered him as was dragged up the wall.

He wondered if he could have done more to save his father's life. The thought had not left him since the moment of realisation that he had caused the death of his father. His insides churned as the thoughts raced round his brain again. He knew his father had saved his cousin Christopher. But also knew his father hazarded his own life to rescue him when he'd been irresponsible by being aboard the *Seagull*.

Fred picked up a collecting tin and stood in front of the lifeboat. He glanced down the road and saw his mother coming, with Kitty clinging to her arm. Fred looked again, not daring to believe his mother had at last left the cottage for the first time since the funeral.

Frank watched his mother approach, and he stood alongside his brother, not daring to speak. All the family thought that Mary had lost her mind with her grief. And he had heard about the rows and recriminations of the townspeople, claiming that it had been unnecessary for his father to die. He'd heard that the lifeboats should not have been launched, just as his father said. But it was all too late. Kit Brown had drowned while saving lives. And Frank Brown knew his father was a hero. He looked up at his brother, and wondered if he, too, would ever wear a deep blue gansey in a lifeboat. Frank tried to imagine what thoughts were going through Fred's mind.

Fred watched a group of people approach the lifeboat. He brushed his eyes with his sleeve, steadied himself on his crutches, held out the collecting tin, and called: "Penny for the lifeboat, penny for the lifeboat."

Frank rattled his box. "Help save a life at sea."

As she watched coins drop into the boxes, a flurry of light rain added to Mary's tears. She shuddered. Kitty Brown looked up at her mother. "Dad's not coming home again, is he, Mam?"

"No, love, he's not."

Fred put an arm round Kitty's shoulders. "But I'll look after you. I'm the man of the house now."